THE GHOST
WHO BLED

GREGORY NORMINTON

First published in Great Britain in 2017 by Comma Press
www.commapress.co.uk

Versions of 'The Poison Tree' and 'Fall Caesar' were broadcast on BBC Radio 4.
'The Ghost Who Bled' was published in *Prospect*, 'The Hermit of Athos' in *The
London Magazine*, 'The Halt' in *Gutter* and 'In My Father's Garden' in *The Lonely
Crowd*. 'The Time Traveller's Breakdown' appeared in *Postscripts 22/23* and
'Confessions of a Tyrant's Double' in *Postscripts 24/25*. 'The Modification of Eugene
Berenger' first appeared in *Bio-Punk* and 'Bottleneck' will be published in *10 Years
Asleep* (forthcoming), both published by Comma Press. 'The Soul Surgeons' featured
in *Book of Voices*, published by Flame Books in support of Sierra Leone PEN.

The story 'Fall Caesar' is based on an idea by Alex Taylor
– to whom this collection is dedicated.

A CIP catalogue record of this book is available from the British Library.

ISBN   1905583567
ISBN-13   978 1905583560

The publisher gratefully acknowledges the support of Arts Council England.

Supported using public funding by
**ARTS COUNCIL
ENGLAND**

Printed and bound in England by CPI Group Ltd

To Alex Taylor

Contents

The Poison Tree

THIS IS A STORY my neighbours told me. I cannot say how much of it is true, for I never knew the participants. I have, however, inhaled fine particles of skin and hair that used to belong to one of them: my predecessor in this house, a man with the perfectly forgettable name of Roger Wilson. It is his part in this story – the story of a friendship – that I feel compelled to set down, as though his ghost were hovering above my shoulder. Yet as well as being a story of friendship, this is a story of hate: hate that grows from indebtedness and becomes a fuel for living.

They sailed from Liverpool to Singapore, two youngsters itching in army cloth, astounded by the tropical heat. Roger Wilson was a private, fresh from grammar school; Frank Lively, a graduate of Sandhurst, was Second Lieutenant in the 1st Battalion Worcestershire Regiment.

They trained in the foul, bone-steaming jungle. Within the bounds of rank they developed a mutual sympathy that swelled to friendship on the unruly ship to Butterworth. From the haze of that industrial port, they were sent out to patrol the headwaters of the Muda River. Roger and Frank were lulled to sleep by the night chorus of frogs and cicadas. They awoke under damp canvas to the siren calls of gibbons and the overhead whoosh of hornbills. The days were a misery of sweat and rot powder; periods of rest revealed the jellied blood left by sated leeches. There was as much talk of pit vipers and

1

scorpions as of the Chinese enemy. This was fear's reticence, for neither British nor Malayan soldier could hope to survive capture.

The platoon was crossing a stream when the ambush happened. Frank Lively, who often spoke with pride of his jungle adventures, remembered the school of leaf-dark fishes and a glassy-eyed toad that swam before their boots; then the crackle of gunfire from the tangled bank. Two soldiers fell. The rest of the platoon, under covering fire, made it to the bank and began a counterattack. One of the fallen was twenty-year-old Jack Harmon, a butcher's boy from Tewkesbury. The other, more fortunate than Private Harmon in that he still lived, was Roger Wilson. Struck in the left thigh, mesmerised by the flow of his blood in the stream, Roger tried to reach the shelter of a fallen tree, but pain and a sudden lassitude kept him exposed in the stream. Only the shock of the water on his face saved him from fainting. Flocks of mud took off from the bank; watery flowers burst open in the stream. A pair of legs kicked water at him. He felt himself being dragged to safety.

Frank Lively's heroics that day went undecorated; his friendship with the man whose life he had saved was recompense enough. The Second Lieutenant visited Private Wilson several times at the military hospital. He confided in Roger about his life and Roger, out of politeness, returned the intimacy. They exchanged addresses before Roger's repatriation and, in the months that followed, several letters came to the hospital in Bordon where Roger was recuperating.

The two met again in 1956, after Frank had resigned his commission. Frank, whose father was someone or other in the City, offered his former comrade a minor post in the merchant bank where he, Frank, had so easily found a position. Roger was reluctant; the debt he owed was already too great. But Frank pish-poshed this nonsense. He insisted, and Roger, who was due to marry soon, accepted the job.

For years they were almost colleagues. Frank accepted the request to play godfather to Roger's daughter. In return,

Margaret Wilson was the matron of honour at the wedding of Frank Lively to his beloved Susan. The friendship between the two couples reached its height in 1960, when Frank seized the chance to buy the house next door to the Wilsons. What better way to live than to choose one's own neighbours?

The souring of the friendship proceeded from this new proximity. Margaret Wilson and Susan Lively shared, in good humour, the burdens of motherhood but their husbands became subtly estranged. The process took many years. By the end of the sixties, Roger was turning down games of golf and declining, with regretful smiles, to pool resources with the Livelys for a joint holiday in Brittany.

There was a new tone in Roger's voice that only his wife detected. 'Frank's in our house too much,' he complained. 'Why must he always have me at hand to remind him of his heroics?' He tried, by paying for tennis lessons, to steer his children towards new friendships, but Roger's boy and Frank's two sons continued to fight their jungle battles in Frank's garden, while Roger's daughter, Dorothy, made up for her lack of a female companion by flirting, from earliest adolescence, with Frank's oldest boy, Ben.

In the baking summer of 1976, this flirtation got out of hand. Roger caught Ben Lively and his daughter lying together amidst the dust motes in her bedroom. The ferocity of his rage shocked everyone, and neighbours on their veldt-yellow lawns peered above withered privet to watch Roger drag the yelping boy to his parents' door.

A war of attrition followed, with Dorothy confined to her sweltering bedroom and Ben baying her name across the cypress hedge. Margaret Wilson tried to reason with her husband but he held firm until the drought broke and Ben, strapping luggage to the roof of his father's car, drove off to Warwick University.

Within a few seasons the children of both households had flown. Dorothy, the original focus of tension, moved, as soon as her schooling was over, to a squatter commune in Brixton.

Roger, to absorb the shame of this disloyalty, turned his attention to a new injustice.

This time it was a gingko tree in Frank's garden. In a bitter letter, Roger objected to the tree's excessive shade. Frank's reply, hand delivered, offered only pitying refutation. The gingko – a Chinese native, as Roger never ceased to observe – was of no great size and incapable of draining, as Roger alleged, all the moisture from the soil. Ah, but the wretched tree starved his side of light: how else to explain Frank's lush garden?

'Yes, lush, it's like a jungle in there,' Roger complained. 'And no wonder it's so green when you consider all the water he wastes – and all the light he takes from *our side.*'

The dispute smouldered for years. The innocent tree, still visible from my study window, came to symbolise all that was poisonous in the men's acquaintance. Roger lopped a single branch that hung above his gardenias, but the long-term goal of a felling went unachieved.

Not long after taking early retirement, Frank Lively suffered his first heart attack. This brought about a truce, even a brief rapprochement, between the neighbours. Frank expressed in oblique terms to his wife his desire for reconciliation. 'How can I forget what we went through,' he said, 'me and Roger, in the jungle?'

Negotiations took place in the respective marital bedrooms. Roger, with his daughter estranged and his son moving to Ontario, fell prey to uncustomary tearfulness. He agreed to supper at their old Italian restaurant.

All went well until the tiramisu, when Frank began to reminisce about Malaya. He had, he said, begun to dream of the ambush and of fallen Private Harmon. Listen, he said, what would Roger say to a return visit? There were affordable flights these days to Singapore. They could pay a visit to Jack Harmon's grave at Kranji War Cemetery.

Roger wound his napkin into a rope and stared at the tablecloth. Illness had made them almost equals, but now

Frank had brought to the feast the terrible subject of Roger's debt: the life he owed to Frank Lively and which he had failed to make remarkable.

Within a minute, the peace negotiated by their respective wives had been torn asunder. Roger could not go back to that green hell. It was a rotten idea. Other diners turned their heads, like ruminants at a watering hole, and there were many witnesses to Roger's retreat from the restaurant, a handful of banknotes uncounted at his place on the table.

Open hostilities were not resumed but Margaret Wilson had to live each day with the unending litany of her husband's grievances. Hatred of the Livelys ought to have weakened Roger, yet in the end it was his wife who succumbed to the acid of his loathing. Her liver became diseased; after diagnosis she faded quickly. Roger was too proud to allow Susan Lively into the bedroom where, propped among pillows, his wife was slipping towards death. He nursed her day and night. Their daughter came back for a while and slept under her parents' roof, until the day came when home care would not be sufficient and Margaret was transferred to a hospice.

In the weeks that followed her death, Roger kept the condolence card addressed to him by Frank and Susan unopened beside the bread bin. He spent each day in the garden seeking order, and at night he left a glass of water on the empty side of the bed. He went on holiday, alone, to Wales and when he returned he gave in to the long-anticipated pleasure of tearing up the condolence card inside its envelope.

The passion of his hatred had no limits. Even when, five years after Margaret's death, Susan in turn succumbed to cancer, Roger continued to nurse his loathing of Frank Lively. The widowers, one of them abandoned by his children, the other adoringly visited at weekends, would acknowledge one another without speaking. They contrived to collect their milk bottles at the same instant; the presence of one pottering about his garden would prompt the other to do the same, and each would kneel within hearing of the other.

Frank never did return to Malaysia. In the summer of 1997, at his younger son's house in Swindon, he suffered a fatal heart attack. Roger Wilson is known to have attended the funeral but he shunned the efforts of the younger Livelys to acknowledge him. Frank's house was quickly sold, and Roger had a new generation of shrieking children to endure. The hated abundance of Frank's garden was grubbed up and replaced with decking. Only the gingko, that vegetable symbol of Roger's obsession, was left as a reminder of all that he had lost.

The story might have ended there, were it not for the stealthy encroachment, on Roger's dreams, of that long-ago jungle. He found himself in his widower's bed sweating and hunted again, waking himself with his cries. Frank Lively's invitation to a voyage still stood; his shade had made it a challenge. Thus, at the age of sixty-seven, and to the surprise of his neighbours, Roger Wilson flew to Singapore and visited the grave of Private Harmon. Thereafter, obeying some inner compulsion, he travelled north to the Malaysian state of Kedah and made his way to the Muda River.

Roger squatted in the middle of a boat, gawping at the trunks of trees drowned many years ago when the river was dammed. Upstream, the same dam and El Niño's protracted dry season had dwindled the river to veins of water between sand bars. Roger was obliged to help drag the boat, his legs in the warm, grit-swirling shallows. He despaired of scaling the green ramparts of the jungle and the expedition was abandoned.

He stopped for five days in a hotel resort outside Kuala Lumpur, only to find that forest fires in Sumatra had cloaked the Malaysian peninsular in sickening brown smog. The city's buildings seemed to dissolve in the haze. Roger tried to rest by the abandoned swimming pool but he felt the pollution fogging up his lungs. The discomfort spread to his belly. Even indoors, under air conditioning, the stink lingered in his nostrils and he suffered pangs like those of constipation. Once, he took a taxi into town, but the monstrous scale of the

Petronas Towers as they loomed through the smog made him nauseous and he asked the driver to turn back.

In the grounds of the hotel, the birds had stopped singing. Even the cicadas were silent.

It was necessary to leave immediately. The smiling, effeminate Indonesians at the desk could not comprehend his urgent speech. He needed, whatever the cost, to catch an earlier plane home, but so many tourists were doing the same that he would have to wait, locked in his gilded cage, for his flight. Fury seized hold of him such as he had not felt since the day he found Ben Lively in his daughter's bedroom. Frank, it was Frank who was to blame. Roger had come out to discharge some part of his debt to him, to defy him also. He had made it so far, only to be thwarted by drought, fire and his own mediocrity. Roger paced in anguish, taking deep breaths of smog under the silent palms.

His lungs began to flood. He choked and fell to his knees on the coarse, tropical lawn. He coughed and groaned, unable to lift his face clear of the stream. A pair of legs rushed towards him. Dry, brown hands gripped his wrists. Roger grimaced and bit for air but the damp earth surged up to claim him.

He let go of a life that had lost all meaning.

Fall Caesar

Between the acting of a dreadful thing
And the first motion, all the interim is
Like a phantasma or a hideous dream.
                                    Julius Caesar, II (i)

PETER DAWSON'S ONSTAGE MURDER was certain to steal the show. He was not naturally a selfish actor: he was, by his colleague's accounts, a joy, a pearl to work with. But certain immutable facts forced his hand, and a lifelong respect for his fellow actors would have to be sacrificed for his final flourish. All actors know about sacrifice: it is the condition of their art and a mark of their courage that, Spartan-like, they comb each other's hair before entering the fray. With his final exit, Peter Dawson would bring the art form to its apogee. Like all theatre, his demise would be fleeting as ice-sculpture yet etched into memory. By the time reality and artifice were untangled – and this would never be entirely feasible – the act would be finished, the die would be cast and one of the cast would be dead.

He sat in a black plastic chair and eyed his reflection; the pasty face of Julius Caesar stared back. He plunged his hand between his legs to stop it trembling. From a corner of the dressing room, a speaker transmitted the murmuring of the early settlers. Peter Dawson feared and loved these strangers: their steady hands on chocolate boxes, their heavy winter coats that smelt of London, their fingers idling through unprescient programmes. Reaching for the powder puff, he recognised in his mouth the bitter-almond taste of fear. What could he expect of them, his audience? What if they got bored; what if they shuffled through his death-throes; what if they just didn't *get* it?

There was a knock at the door. Peter Dawson, unprepared for the sight of Gary Mendus in tunic, cloak and sandals, reacted pertly. 'You look like you're wearing a nappy.'

Mendus shrugged. 'You're the one needs nappies.'

'What?'

'When you die you shit yourself.'

'Don't tell me that now. I don't want to know that now.'

'You call this Method acting?'

'Look, what are you doing in my dressing-room?'

Mendus scratched his massive thigh. 'I'm nervous.'

'What?'

'It's all right for you, I never been onstage before.'

'Well I've never died before, am I complaining?'

'Cheers for the support.'

'Look, once you're onstage and acting – or in your case, reacting – everything will be fine. The nerves will vanish. You'll enjoy it.'

Mendus implored the heavens with greasy, butcher's palms. 'I'm used to working a little more private, you know.'

'Christ, it's simple: when I say, *Doth not Brutus bootless kneel*, Casca says –'

'*Speak, hands, for me* – Yeah, we've gone over it.'

'Then you've nothing to fear.'

'Unlike you.'

Peter eyed the man reproachfully. 'You needn't be brutal about it.'

'That's exactly what I need to be.'

Peter shut his eyes and tried to focus on his breath.

'I don't like the way some of the actors are looking at me. That one off *Casualty*,' said Mendus, 'asked me who I was.'

'Well they won't challenge you on stage. Where in

Shakespeare is the line, *Did I see you in rehearsals?* Just move as we rehearsed. Mingle with the conspirators and when they come in for the –'

'Stabbing'

'You leave me on the stage and over the speeches that follow, you vanish into the night.'

Gary Mendus frowned. He stroked the edge of his dagger in anxious thought. 'You got any acting tips, then?'

'*No.*'

'Pff.'

'Now if you don't mind, I'd like to prepare in peace.'

Peter Dawson could feel Gary Mendus' hurt behind him. He did not look up as the man withdrew and left him with his imminent end.

Two weeks earlier, he had sat in the consultation room hearing nothing. The doctor, a shrimpish, gingery Scot with red mottled hands, spoke clearly and kindly to Peter Dawson's left ear. 'Of course, it can take months for the tumour seriously to impair your movements. You may still be active at Christmas. But sooner or later, I'm afraid, you'll have to resign yourself.'

Peter Dawson struggled to fasten onto these words. They swept past him like leaves in a storm. He felt intense sympathy for the pink little man before him, for the raw hands as they slept on the desk.

'How long do I have?'

'No more than six months.'

'Six months starting when, exactly?'

'Starting now.'

'When you say now, or when I say now?'

A tiny ripple travelled across the doctor's face. His hands yawned and stretched. He took a deep breath. 'I'll prescribe you something to help with anxiety. Do you have anyone to go back to?'

The doctor placed a hand on his shoulder. Peter glimpsed the ring and caught the wifely smell of lavender soap. 'I'm very sorry,' he said to the hand, and found himself at school again, longing for his mother.

The auditorium was filling up fast. The cast had assembled in the corridor and was pacing through its warm-ups. Faces stretched and shrank; lips splayed and puckered; lungs expanded. Peter Dawson ran to the toilet.

'Are you in here?' he wheezed. 'Where the hell are you?'

Feet shuffled in the cubicle. Gary Mendus' head appeared above the partition. 'What do you want? I'm *preparing*.'

Peter wet his lips. On the tannoy, Flavius and Marullus chid the fickle crowd. 'Look, I've been thinking –'

'You're on in a minute.'

'Yes, yes –'

'There'll be panic in the wings. "Where's Caesar when you need him?"'

'Listen –'

'You got the first *line*, ain't ya?'

Peter staggered and spun. 'Stay here,' he said. 'Don't move till I return.'

'The line is *Calpurnia – Calpurnia*.'

'Goddamit, I know,' said Peter.

But he forgot.

Act One, Scene Two, did not pass off as he would have wished for a valedictory performance. In the corridor, Calpurnia eyed him strangely and Mark Antony arched a well-trained eyebrow.

'Have you seen – ?' said Peter.

'Hm?'

'Oh never mind.'

Peter Dawson pulled the curtain behind him and fell into his chair. His make-up was running slowly into his eyes; usually it stayed the distance. He looked at the pasty face in the mirror and noted, without the cold eye he might have wished for, the pitted texture of his skin and the bags under his eyes like bruises on fruit. He saw the depressingly thin lips, his father's, that were to disappear with him. His guts clenched: in his death he was finally killing his parents.

He jumped to his feet and rooted through his rucksack for a flask of malt whisky. He gripped the flask until his knuckles whitened. No: he was going to persevere. He hadn't risked arrest, hadn't spent ten terrible minutes explaining himself to that terrifying man, only to bottle it at the last and die slowly, humiliatingly and without an audience, a mere six months hence. He had lived a good life – had, in a sense, lived many lives on stage, and it was on stage that his story should end. The whisky burned his chest. He extracted the briefcase from under the dressing table and peered inside. It seemed, come to think of it, an inordinately large sum for the task. Still, the market decides, there being no precedents in his favour. Stoically, he returned the cash to its hiding-place. Gary Mendus knew where his payment lay: there would just be time, afterwards, to snatch it and run. How he made it from there to his retirement under a tropical sun was the man's own damn business.

Peter's stomach flinched again and, with great reluctance, he passed wind. He stood for a moment enjoying the miasma; and began to sob. He sobbed at first for his body, for the close companionship of bowels, of kidneys, of liver and spleen. He sobbed for his skin, for the bacteria that sloughed off his former selves particle by particle. He wept for the blood cells that, even now, were passing through against the dark cloud in his skull.

He sat down and, with the hem of his toga, dried his eyes. Life was still worth it. He wanted every minute, every second, even the last. He wanted to go on breathing, to cherish every gulp of lovely air. He wanted time to read at least a few more books, to hear just once his favourite sonata, his most cherished song. What madness, what farce: to die as someone else, to thrill the crowd and know the crowd deluded. The test of faith had come and gone; he had emerged triumphant. Goddamit, where was Mendus?

Nineteen minutes later, he found him hulking in the wings, at a slight remove from the actors. Sweating thickly, half-delirious with panic, Peter shuddered up to him.

'Where *were* you?'

Mendus barely blinked. 'Keeping out of sight.'

'I've been looking all over for you.'

'Yeah?'

'Yes I bloody have.'

Mendus seized Peter by the toga. 'Now look, you hired a professional. Don't get at me for my doing my job.'

'That's just it. I'm cancelling the hit.'

'What?'

'I'm pulling the plug. I'm calling it off.'

'What about my money?'

'What about it?'

'I've got my retirement to think about.'

'Oh God, oh God.'

Behind them, senators hissed for silence. 'Shut up,' one said.

'You shut up.'

'Be *quiet*.'

Portia's monologue was coming to a close and the senators strained in their sandals. Peter Dawson trembled. He stared from stage to hitman, from hitman to stage. What was he waiting for? Let the man have his cash. What was money when life was at stake? He turned to Gary Mendus and tugged his sleeve. 'Would you consider a cancellation fee?'

There was a loud, braying flourish, the lighting changed and Peter was swept up in a tide of white togas. He strained briefly against his fellow actors, encountering resistance. 'The Ides of March are come,' he said, casting about him. Mendus had disappeared. Characters spoke and gestured. Mendus was gone: so it was understood: the contract was revoked. Peter Dawson breathed deeply; calmer now, he moved into gear. He was in his element. The heat of the stage-lights, the darkened breathing auditorium, were to him like water to a gasping fish. The thrill of commanding such attention oxygenated his oppressed brain. He moved, and listened to the fine sonorities of his cherished baritone.

Then Metellus spoke, then Brutus. Julius Caesar answered and down the steps the conspirators came. Peter spoke the lines as, nightmare-like, his nemesis emerged from behind a pillar. In all the other senators, a bloody intent was sheathed in smiles. Not so this one. Peter's blood thrilled with terror. As in a dream he heard himself intone the poetry of fatal hubris:

> The skies are painted with unnumbered sparks,
> They are all fire, and every one doth shine;
> But there's but one in all doth hold his place.
> So in the world: 'tis furnished well with men,
> And men are flesh and blood, and apprehensive —

He hesitated, seeing tension in the senators' eyes that shone black like berries. The air was keen with anticipation. His heart thumped hard with pride.

> Yet in the number I do know but one
> That unassailable holds on his rank,
> Unshaked of motion; and that I am he
> Let me show it, even in this —

Now he glared defiantly at Mendus, his lip curled in a sneer of cold command:

> That I was constant Cimber should be banished,
> And constant do remain to keep him so.

In seconds the last lines evaporated. Casca's mouth opened and shut noiselessly; he brandished his blade and Peter shrank back. Suddenly he recalled his will, his desperate need to live. But it was too late, the plastic daggers tickled his sides. His eyes cast about for someone who might save him. All they found was a wall of hating faces: Brutus, Cassius, Casca, Cinna. And there was Mendus, arm aloft, deaf to protestation. Caesar put out his hands in self-defence and, fluffing his line, he died.

Zero + 30

THE JOURNEY TOOK SEVEN hours and several weeks off Henry's life – or so it felt, as their driver dodged potholes and craters and ruffled the hides of browsing cattle. It ought to have been a relief to stop; yet when they refuelled in a dirt-track town, a cloud of dragonflies simmered above their vehicle and they were instantly surrounded by beggars. Vaing stared at the front headrest, having first checked that the doors were locked, but when an amputee caressed Henry with his stump through the open window, they had to scrabble for some riel notes to get rid of him. Henry sweated as small brown fingers tapped against the glass, and sighed with relief when their driver returned to swat the children away.

'Two more hours,' translated Vaing as they set off once more with a blast of horns. She took a bottle of mineral water from their rucksack and tipped the contents sparingly over her headscarf; then she rolled the headscarf into a band and set it around her husband's head. He laughed, protesting, but the damp material cooled him and took the edge off his travel sickness.

He had been dreading this trip into the countryside. The capital had been full enough of ghosts, though the family home had made way for a charcoal factory and the garden where, as a child, his wife used to play was now a lumber yard. Still, in the city it had been possible to act as tourists, and when Vaing wasn't obeying some inner imperative to seek out lost places, Henry had kept them busy with sightseeing. They had visited the Royal Palace – 'royer palair', as their five-dollar guide called it – and Henry had photographed, with a kind of manic diligence, the gilded pavilions and potted plants and the garish murals crumbling in the heat. Chinese and Vietnamese tourists posed before the pagodas; Henry imagined that they accepted more readily than he did the presence of limbless beggars outside the palace walls, and the children who drifted along the lakefront selling pirated books.

'If you buy one,' Vaing had said as they watched the boys ply their trade, 'you will have to buy several.'

'So what? I can afford it.'

But the exchange that took place in the comfort of an absurdly overpriced café turned sour when, catching on to the success of their colleague, other young hawkers began to stroke Henry's arms and whimper.

'Told you,' said Vaing; yet she too bought a book (in French, the language that would once have killed her) and refused the change that her boy reached for.

Her hand, now, in the jolting car, settled on Henry's thigh. He felt the tremor in her fingers and tried to still it with his sweating paw. 'Do you recognise anything?' he said. Vaing had lost her brother on the forced march to the village. He had been taken into the bushes and killed with a hoe; the soldiers were not supposed to waste bullets.

'I can't tell,' she said. How could she hope to recognise the place? It was flat, monotonous country, worked hard by the plough, with here and there the gaudy interruption of a temple curling above the flood; the Mekong had broken its banks, fish were swimming in the treetops and all that could be moved had come to higher ground alongside the road. Henry photographed the drowned pastures, the thatched misery of dwellings that friends back home would call picturesque. The huts on stilts that followed the road, connected to dry land by rickety wooden ramps, made him think of chicken coops.

He looked in vain for elderly faces.

Vaing's head fell sleeping against his shoulder five minutes before they arrived. The driver parked, opened his door to suck on a cigarette and waggled his gas-pedal foot as if to shake out the madness that had possessed it. Henry paid, roused his wife and carried their luggage into the cool interior of the hotel.

As soon as they had settled into their room, Vaing surprised her husband by suggesting a stroll. Thirty years ago, she and others had been marched directly to the village, bypassing this town, so that its languorous existence beside the Mekong held no terror for her.

A drab compound beside their hotel turned out to be a monastery, its windows draped with orange and saffron robes. Henry signalled to a young monk and asked Vaing to interpret for them. Her hands met in salutation before the stripling; having asked about the monastery, they learned that its abbot was only 28 years old. Vaing had not set foot in Cambodia in all the days of his life.

They found a congenial café run by a skinny American, and after a good supper – that must have cost half a month's local wages – they walked back to the hotel. Vaing took a diazepam, but Henry lay under the ceiling's juddering fan unable to sleep. For most of their life together it had been the other way round, with Vaing marooned in wakefulness while her husband snored beside her. In the first days of their acquaintance she had kept her insomnia from him. '*C'est à cause des rêves,*' she had explained finally, on their last night in Bangkok before he brought her home to Cleveland to be his bride.

In the early years they used to communicate in French, and somehow the medium of a foreign language softened, for Henry at least, the magnitude of the ordeal she had lived through. With time, however, as her English improved and she became acclimatised to her new homeland, he had had to accommodate his wife's nightmares, her shrinking suspicion of loud people at parties, her abhorrence of confinement. More difficult – for Henry was a fastidious housekeeper – was her habit of hoarding freebies, from salt sachets and hotel pens to promotional gimmicks delivered in the mail. Every so often, even now, he would have to get up in the night and empty the drawers that she had filled with things they would never need.

It had taken him years to coax her into a therapist's office. At first she had spoken of her past as though it had occurred to an acquaintance; only gradually, as she reconciled herself to the sessions and began to bring their discoveries home, did Henry learn about the capture of Phnom Penh and the horrors that followed. The forced march; the terror of revealing any kind of schooling; the exhaustion of working in paddy fields on starvation rations; the perils of falling asleep during indoctrination sessions – all these things Vaing had recounted with a semblance of calm. She told him how she and three others had been apprised of their imminent execution; how, in the confusion that followed the Vietnamese invasion, they had fled the camp and set off on a gruelling haul through jungle into Thailand. One of her friends had lost her life after stepping on a landmine. Another companion, who lived now in Ottawa, had almost to be carried by the end, so weakened was she by malaria and dysentery. Vaing herself had suffered weeping sores whose scars had kept her, for 30 years, from baring her legs in public.

Absorbing these accounts in the lamp-lit privacy of his den, Henry had raged at his powerlessness to annul his wife's pain, to participate in her grief for her murdered parents – as if by sharing he might have diminished the burden. To compensate for what, in his guiltier or more indulgent moments, he considered his empathic failure, Henry read books, watched documentaries. For years, saying little about it to his wife, he studied the wretched history of her country – in which his own had played a sinister part. Henry knew how many Cambodians had died in Kissinger's bombing raids; he recoiled physically each time he saw the bastard on TV, tapped as an elder statesman for his opinion on terrorism, homeland security, Iran. Vaing did not share Henry's outrage; or if she did, she kept it to herself. 'He's on TV,' she would say, 'he can't hear you getting mad at him.'

In the shuttered darkness of their hotel room, Henry's wife shifted onto her side and murmured. He watched her sleeping form. Though aging like him and with more health problems, she could still, without conscious effort, make him catch his breath. The elegance of her simplest movements made him feel oafish in comparison. Still, she conferred the honour of her grace upon him. He knew that he would never meet such another.

At last, feeling sleep begin to tug at him, with a wisp of her hair stirring in the fan's breath, Henry closed his eyes; and he suffered, without the usual anxiety of resistance, the observation that, while his wife's love was like home to him, he could never be entirely a home to his wife.

★

The next day, Vaing was tense and introspective. Henry asked if she would prefer to return to Phnom Penh; it would be no dishonour to avoid the place where she had suffered. Vaing said, 'I want to see the market,' whereupon Henry dashed into action, gathering his hat and camera and caulking his skin with insect repellent.

The market was a warren of tents, a medley of medieval stink and seeming disorder. Stalls overlapped one another as though competing for light; mothers as they stood by their wares bathed their babies; meat and viscera hung, peppered with flies. Henry watched his wife inspect a bowl of foul-smelling fish paste. 'It's like a furnace in here,' he said. 'I'm going out for some air.'

In the street, Henry breathed slowly to regain his composure. He stood for a time, ogled by barefoot children, under the sign of a dress shop, admiring its florid and heraldic Khmer. Vaing had never encouraged him to make sense of the language; indeed, she had lived so long in English that she complained of difficulty understanding what Cambodians said to her.

'Does that bother you?' he'd asked, days earlier, in the capital.

'Why should it?'

If they had had children, the language might have been revived for her in passing it on. That old regret – not a searing pain now, but the cold pang of a contained sadness – passed through him like a ghost.

Swift bodies brushed past him, jolting him from a stupor. Troubled, he felt for the camera at his hip and found it gone. Sweat descended like a mask across his face. He called Vaing's name and searched for her among the stalls. In the end she found him. She had bought wafer biscuits and sticky rice cake.

'My camera's been stolen.'

'Are you sure?'

'I had it slung over my shoulder. Someone must have taken it.'

They returned to the hotel, Henry cursing his inattentiveness. Vaing spoke to reception and, within minutes, a plainclothes policeman came to find them. The man was handsome, tall for a Cambodian, his hair slicked back with pomade. Vaing explained as best she could what had happened, and the police officer treated her husband to looks of concern and sympathy before assuring him, with placid conviction, that the camera would be returned.

'How can you be so confident?'

'No problem,' said the police officer. Smiling, he repeated the English phrase as though he had just invented it. 'No problem' propelled him, with neat bows and a handshake for Henry, across the terrace and down the steps into the street.

'Nice guy. Can't imagine he's serious though.'

'I'm tired,' said Vaing. 'I'm going to take a nap.'

He was alone for an hour, which he spent in the lounge, relishing the cool breath of a fan and watching the traffic along the bank of the Mekong. The far side of the flood was perhaps a mile off, a sombre line of green. He dozed in the heat and started at his own snore. Vaing found him and together they lunched on rice and the knobbliest parts of a chicken. Vaing loved to gnaw skin, cartilage: what Henry called the scruff and knuckles. She mocked him for his squeamishness. 'I don't have your teeth,' he protested: the irony being that his were exemplary, a marvel of American dentistry. Well, he liked to joke, it pays to advertise. He had begun to practise before they met. Back in '79, a fully qualified orthodontist, he had volunteered for the Peace Corps: a matter of living a little, of severing also the umbilical cord at the late age of thirty-two.

His mother had been dead now for 18 months. Vaing was his only family.

'Listen,' he said. 'Why don't we just go now? Hire a taxi and see the place, look around, get the hell out. Come back here in time for supper – make a restful night of it.'

'No,' said Vaing.

'What are we waiting for?' Her lips compacted; he watched her chicken-greased fingers clench. 'I don't mean to bully you.'

'It's not... Henry, I need time.'

'Of course.'

'We will go.'

'Only if you want to.'

'But not today.'

'Okay.'

'Not today.'

★

They were eating breakfast on the terrace the next morning when the police officer came to find them. He presented Henry with his camera and stepped back from the table as an artist might to admire his handiwork. Henry was agog, effusive with thanks. Vaing, less impressed, folded her napkin and spoke in a soft voice to the police officer. While the two conversed, Henry checked to his satisfaction that the camera was still in working order.

'He says a boy stole it,' said Vaing.

'A street kid?'

'A boy with a dying mother.'

Henry looked for confirmation from the lean, pomaded officer. The man waved a hand as though chasing a fly and Vaing translated: 'They have him in custody. He's a known thief.'

'How old is he?'

'Fifteen.'

'What will happen to him?'

Vaing inquired. 'Prison.'

'And what's the matter with his mother?'

'She has cancer.'

Henry spoke quickly, quietly, as though he feared the man might understand him: 'I don't want this kid going to prison on our account. What if we don't press charges?'

The police officer addressed himself to Henry. Vaing sat back against her chair and the look on her face was a blend of sarcasm and vindication. 'He says,' she explained, 'that we will have to pay for this to happen.'

'For what? The boy to go free?'

'We will have to pay.'

Henry, appalled, managed to keep an impassive expression. 'This is a set-up.'

'You want to leave the kid where he is?'

'Oh no. Jesus.' Henry reached into his back pocket and extracted his wallet. The police officer feigned indifference and watched the river traffic. Vaing asked how much and he relayed the sum to her uncomprehending husband. It was the cost of a good meal in a restaurant back home. Henry placed the riel notes in the placid open palm.

'The boy stole from us,' said Henry when the police officer had gone, 'and we pay for his freedom.'

'I could have told you,' said Vaing. It reminded Henry of the sparrows in Phnom Penh. On their first stroll from the compound of their hotel, they had found themselves on the esplanade with other western tourists. Lean men were displaying sparrows in cages: so many, they churned behind the bars. The idea was to exchange a few riels for a sparrow's freedom. Henry had obliged, despite Vaing's objections, and minutes later, on a grassy square in front of the palace, they found that boys were stunning the liberated birds with pellets from slings, then pocketing them and returning them to their cages.

Vaing wiped rice grains from her skirt. 'Where are you going,' asked Henry.

'To clean my teeth. Then I want to read that book I bought.'

'Are we not –?'

'Henry, I want to read.'

Another day dragged by. Henry strolled alongside the river, sweat tickling his back and forming a marsh between his breasts. He took photographs and smiled amiably at the people who crossed his path. He showed small children their faces in the digital screen: their lithe fingers clambered over his as they vied to see themselves. He wandered to the edge of town, rested in the shade of a tapang tree, then trudged wearily back to the procrastination of his wife.

At the end of a sweltering afternoon, a thunderstorm broke. Rainwater fell in cords from the eaves of the hotel. Henry lost his temper.

'We can't stay here forever, Vaing, our flight's in two days – we have to get back to Phnom Pen.'

Vaing did not raise her voice like her husband. She put up instead a wall of resistance: what Henry's mother used to call, to her son in private, her Veil of Oriental Inscrutability. 'We still have time,' she said at last.

'I feel I'm pressuring you. Like I keep saying, if you really don't think it can help –'

'*Help*,' said Vaing. 'That's your word. Are you looking for me to find closure?'

'I guess that's the idea.'

'It's nonsense.'

'Then why did we come?'

Vaing looked at her husband: the light was failing, the world beyond their window a tumult of thunder and rain, yet he could see the anguish in her face. 'To see what remains,' she said. 'Because the place is still there. And so in my dreams am I.' He reached across the mattress for her hand. 'Just don't use the modish phrases.'

'I promise.'

'Because that's something I *really* can't face. Not now I'm here.'

She turned away from him and Henry lay still, listening for the change in his wife's breathing. He bent his right arm above his head and pressed his cheek into the cool of his bicep, to soothe himself with his own touch.

'Tomorrow,' said Vaing. 'We will go to the village tomorrow.'

★

Their hotel had prepared for them a packed lunch of greasy omelettes in baguettes. Henry could not imagine having an appetite but he stowed them in his backpack along with water and aspirin.

They had booked a cab to take them the few miles to the village where Vaing had been held prisoner. The driver leaned on his horn as though he could not trust the horse-drawn carts or multi-occupant scooters to notice them. 'Feels like we're part of a motorcade,' said Henry. He squeezed his wife's knee. 'Are you okay?'

'I'm okay.'

They watched the road and the drowned fields: fruit trees and bushes and tangles of bamboo rising from mud-brown waters. Vaing spoke tonelessly to the driver, and Henry, sweating in apprehension, felt almost affronted by the brevity of their journey – as though their occupancy of the jolting SUV had been a bulwark between them and their destination.

It was a poor farming village of thatched huts sprawling along high ground, the road an isthmus where people and livestock clung to the dry. A group of children gathered to watch the white man and the lady in sunglasses step out of their vehicle. A placid mongrel, flea-ridden to judge from its scratching, sniffed at their fingertips.

Henry attempted to gauge, beneath her shades, what passed through his wife's head. She walked slowly as the heat dictated, her arms with their outward, graceful sway unhurried. He felt unequal to the task of upholding her; not that she seemed to need his attentions, closing in on the lone building of stained concrete, its temple-like gate of blackened and corrupted wood.

'Was it here?'

Vaing nodded slowly. She stopped and, hugging herself, looked down the driveway. The building seemed abandoned to Henry but Vaing told him that, according to an inscription in stencilled white paint, it was a warehouse for agricultural machine parts.

'Do you want to go in?'

'I don't own a tractor,' said Vaing. She gave a rumpled smile. 'Henry, will you go wait by the car?'

'What?'

'Just wait for me. I won't be long.'

'I think I should come with you.'

'Do you see that house over there?'

Henry followed her finger to a dismal shack. 'Yes,' he said.

'That was the home of Mrs Seng. I want to find out if she's still there.'

'It's been so long.'

She gave him a peck on the cheek. 'Wait for me by the car.'

Henry walked some little way to give a good impression. When he saw that Vaing had her back turned, he changed course and retraced his steps. This was concern, prudence; it wasn't spying. He breathed heavily, the sweat pooling in his navel as he watched, from behind a screen of tethered cows, the expected disappointment of the woman he loved. Mrs Seng was known to him: not in person, yet he could have recounted to anyone willing to listen how, in the blistering days of his wife's 're-education', an illiterate mother of three, wife herself of a Khmer Rouge soldier – a woman who had nothing to gain from the gesture and everything, life and children included, to lose by it – had several times waved Vaing to a concealed gap in the barbed wire fence, there to slip into the feverish hands of an enemy of the people a hardboiled egg from one of her hens. These Vaing had eaten, under the cover of darkness, scoffing them before a guard could see. The extra protein, not to mention the kindness which found no echo in the brutal round of paddy field, indoctrination and diseased sleep, gave Vaing, in her opinion then and ever after, just enough strength to survive her ordeal and, at the last, to escape it.

Henry watched, one hand flicking at flies, while his wife ascended the wooden steps of the shack. Surely there was little chance of Mrs Seng replying. It had been thirty years: the woman might not have survived the regime, or a combination of disease and poverty would have carried her off long ago. Still, Henry found he was holding his breath – letting it out the instant a small, elderly woman with bottle-top spectacles appeared in the entrance. The woman looked myopically at her visitor. Henry saw her munching, dwindled mouth. She listened with an expression of bewilderment as Vaing spoke, appeared to recoil for an instant, as if dismayed, then placed her arms gently, as one might a necklace of flowers, about his wife's neck. Vaing, perhaps a foot taller, had to crouch into the embrace. Henry could not see his wife's expression – her back was turned – but as Mrs Seng relinquished her hold he could tell that the old woman was crying. She took charge of her visitor's hands and appeared to study them as if they contained something. Holding them still, the old woman led their owner into the obscurity of her shack.

The entrance gaped dimly. A pig squealed somewhere in indignation or terror. Henry regarded the swishing tails of the cows, the flies that made their flanks shudder. He left his hiding-place.

Walking back along the road, Henry found himself an object of curiosity. Naked children stamping in a puddle stopped to watch him. Two youths playing pool on a rough pool table – its baize mangy, the cushions eroded – under a shelter of plastic and thatch, caught his eye and grinned. In another mood Henry might have taken this generously: he had noticed how Cambodian faces could look severe at rest, only to be transformed, *humanised* was the word he dared not utter, by a smile of fellow feeling. Yet he was in a dark mood, too sapped by self-doubt to credit benevolence in others. He doubted his usefulness to his wife. He doubted his moral manhood.

Back at the car, the driver raised an eyebrow. 'She's coming,' said Henry and the driver shrugged. Henry watched the man curl up in his seat for a nap. He watched a balding hen pick dead insects from the SUV's bumper. He felt his resolve fail and walked back as far as the old warehouse.

Flies crawled over his face and neck. He watched the shack and its sun-bleached timbers. The same sun beat down on Henry. It boiled him in his sweat and he was happy to burn, to deliquesce in the place where his wife had suffered. Minutes passed this way, until the scrutiny of locals made him feel a fool and he sought the shade of a tamarind on the other side of the road.

Henry leaned against the tree, trying to look nonchalant. He bent, spraying the dust with his sweat, and picked up a handful of tamarisk husks. He was turning these over, picking them apart, when he saw his wife again.

She was in the road with Mrs Seng. The old woman was holding Vaing's hand and Henry could see that all was not right. What could he have understood of their parting? He waited for Vaing to reach him and unpeeled himself from the tree trunk.

'What happened?'

'I need to keep moving.'

'We'll leave.'

'I don't want to get in the car.'

'Then we can walk.'

'I don't want to *walk*, I just…' Vaing rubbed her arm, looking up and down the road. She moved, fractionally but enough, from his solicitous touch.

'That was Mrs Seng?'

'Nuon.'

'Her name's Nuon?'

'And I saw someone else.'

'Who?'

There was a tremor in Vaing's throat; her mouth was oddly jarred. 'I saw Chey Sok.'

'Are you sure?'

'She's living right next door. They're neighbours.'

In an attempt to calm their nerves, Henry walked his wife as far as the last houses.

'Mrs Seng remembered me. She recognised me. Took me inside like I was her daughter. She has nothing, Henry – she lives on nothing. I wanted to give her some money but she wouldn't take it. Mostly we sat in silence. She didn't even think to warn me. She took me outside. Showed me her vegetable patch. The chickens. And then across. Across.' She clamped her lips until they blanched. 'There was Chey Sok watching us. Old, almost no teeth. But I knew who she was.'

'Did she know you?'

'No. Why would she? I was one of so many.'

Henry swept the perspiration from his face. 'Did you have an exchange?'

'It was just a glance. I thought my heart would stop.'

'What a country,' Henry said, but kept it under his breath. The good unrewarded, the bad unpunished, obliged to live together as if nothing had ever happened.

'You know she was the worst of them.'

'I know,' he said. Three decades of her waking in a sweat beside him, convinced that harsh voice was quacking beside her pillow. 'I don't imagine there's anything we can do.'

'Do?'

'In terms of the law.'

The eyes she turned on him were void of all tenderness. 'You mean like a trial? Take her to court?'

'She committed crimes.'

'She was just a guard. One of thousands.'

'Let's get out of here.'

'You want all this to mean something.'

'Well don't you?'

'I was not raised in America. I don't expect things to work out just because I want them to.'

Henry accompanied her to the cab, where on the ride home she trembled and he held her hand.

Vaing swallowed a pill at the hotel and went to bed for the afternoon. Henry telephoned his receptionist in Cleveland for the benefit of a familiar voice. After sitting out an abrupt sunset in the empty bar, he had drunk just enough to find himself swaying in the darkness above their hotel bed. He heard Vaing stir and take in her waking breath. 'Henry?'

He nodded and sat on the mattress. 'It's dark out.'

'Have long have I been asleep?'

'You were tired. Don't worry about it.' The sheet, just visible in the moonlight, was a landscape that divided them; he contemplated its hills and valleys.

'Is that beer?' said Vaing.

'I'm sorry,' Henry whispered. 'I'm sorry to do this now...'

'What's the matter?'

'Vaing – when I met you in Thailand. When we met at the camp – did you take to me?'

Vaing reached for a glass on the bedside table. He listened to her drinking. 'What are you asking exactly?'

'I want to know why you came with me.'

'Why do you think?'

'I don't dare imagine.'

'Henry,' said Vaing. He dreaded the calm, the clarity in her voice. 'When westerners came to the camp, many women looked to seduce them. It meant a way out – to a better life.'

'And how about me?'

Vaing was silent, her head bowed, and the darkness between them filled for Henry with a panic that seemed to singe his lungs. 'I married you to get away. I didn't think about love: what did *that* mean?'

'And when we got to the States, you planned to leave me?'

'I don't know. Perhaps.'

'Oh Jesus.'

'Henry. I stayed, didn't I?'

'Oh Christ.'

'I'm still here.'

Henry's mouth was parched: he groped in vain for a bottle of mineral water. 'And love?' he said.

'What can I say? Maybe I didn't have it left in me. Maybe it stayed out here – like those women.'

'Do you think if I'd been more...?' He paused to elicit a response.

'More?'

'I guess I always wanted to be strong for you. Carry you.'

'I carried myself through the jungle.'

Henry rubbed his nascent jowls. He knew there was a part of masochism in him and perhaps that was responsible for this inner indictment, his sudden conviction that he had forced Vaing to mother *him* in place of the children she had never borne.

'Henry,' Vaing said, 'you have walked beside me. That's a lot, don't you think?'

'I don't know.'

'We've been alone together. That's better than being alone with no one.'

Henry wanted – he so wanted – to fall into the bed, to curl about his wife's body, his lips pressed to her nape. She sat before him in the moonlight. He could feel the pressure of her gaze on his face. He would have to make do with that: his image in the eyes of a survivor.

In Refugium

1

IN THE AFTERMATH OF the football game, frat houses along the road pounded out their tribal rhythms. There were astounding quantities of litter — food buckets, candy wrappers, drooling drink cans — that Martha Lutz haughtily ignored. At the entrance to the courts, she skipped to avoid a pink Rorschach blot of vomit. 'You'll have to be gentle with me,' she said, as I absorbed a static shock from the gate, 'I'm horribly out of practice.'

Two men were warming up on the court next to ours. Martha waggled her fingers in greeting and the men hailed her. How blithely she staked her claim on the court, stretching like a dancer and arching her back so that her belly button peeped out from under her tee-shirt. She was — oh — the loveliest economist in America: dark, toned and tanned, her erect, almost severe posture combining with a feminine softness of gesture to inflame my homesick senses. I bashed the fluff out of the new balls. Take that, desire; take *that*.

'You serve, John.'

I wasn't going to argue: best get the humiliation out of the way. On my fourth throw (the previous three had sent me reaching for the off-course ball like a man on stilts), I managed it straight and struck the ball heavily into the net. My second service was all timidity, a coquettish swipe inches from my head. The ball ambled over the net and Martha swept towards it. Relieved to have avoided a double fault, I relaxed. A fluorescent blur, a whiffle of breeze, and I beheld

33

the ball strike the netting behind me.

'Love fifteen,' cried Martha. I saw her hop, mindful of her focus, as I returned from chasing the ball. Her black hair had been shaken loose; her breasts stirred in their sports bra.

My first serve sent the ball careening beyond the baseline. My second was a cunning drop shot, but the ball bounced higher than I'd intended and Martha, anticipating its feeble velocity, was already at the net. She curtseyed to launch a volley and my exasperated stretch for an irretrievable return was given voice on the neighbouring court.

'*Nem!*'

I looked over to see a bald, bespectacled and very hairy man toss his racket in the air.

'What's the score?' I asked, though I knew the answer. I considered doing a Michael Chang and serving underarm. From Michael Chang, of course, it had been desperate heroics; from me it would just be pitiful.

'*Nem,*' yelled our neighbour again, and '*Szemét!*' Martha and I watched the man expend his ire on his tennis shoes, beating the soles with his racket head. His opponent, a genial bearded academic, offered us a shrug.

I bounced our ball, leaning over it like a professional. Something fluttered above my head. I looked up.

'Christ!'

A green thing as long as my hand was hurtling towards me in a sickening spiral. It was some kind of insect, a monster locust or mega cicada. In a panic, I swiped at it with my racket.

'What in the hell are you doing?' yelled Martha.

'I'm under attack. Jesus.' I squealed and heard a dull *crump* as racket-head and insect collided. In a sweat I scanned the ground for my enemy. Something stirred on my racket: I tossed it away like a stick of dynamite.

'Wait! Do not harm!'

The hairy foreigner – leaving his service area undefended – dashed across the courts. 'Werry beautiful mantis,' he said, grimacing to reveal a set of milk teeth in a shiny mouthguard of pink gum. 'Quite innocent, if you are not also insect.' He knelt like a suitor beside the twitching monster and coaxed it onto his hand. 'A praying mantis: *Stagmomantis carolina*. It is a relative of cockroach but much more useful.'

'Sorry,' I said, 'it rather panicked me.'

The stranger giggled and squirmed. 'Feet werry prickly. Like thorns of glass.'

'Shards of glass?'

'You say shard? I am still learning.'

His bearded opponent joined us and Martha introduced everyone. 'Peter Danforth,' she said, 'this is John Loyner, my new colleague for the semester.'

'Oh, say.' We shook hands, producing an audible squelch of sweaty palms. Peter Danforth gazed at the mantis on the foreigner's wrist. 'Is Laszlo giving you an entomology lesson?'

'I am entomologist,' said Laszlo.

'Do you study mantises?'

'My main interest is cricket. *Meconoma thalassinum* especially. But I know a little about most insects.'

'He knows,' corrected Peter Danforth, 'everything about all insects.'

Laszlo shook his head. 'Sadly impossible.'

Peter Danforth was also a scientist. 'Artificial Intelligence. What we call empathic systems.'

'Is she not delicious?' the entomologist said. The rest of us peered dubiously at the mantis.

'It looks,' I said, 'like Miles Davis when he made *Bitches Brew*.'

'Often, when mantid emerges in spring, his first meal is sibling.'

There was nothing to add to this. Martha straightened a pleat in her skirt. 'How's Kirsten?' she asked Peter Danforth.

'Hot and bothered and complaining about the kicks. It seems we have a soccer player on the way.'

'Many species look like ant when hatched.'

'Will you give her and junior my best wishes?'

'Surely.'

'But later they *moult*.'

'Laszlo – shall we get back to the game?'

The entomologist cast me a look of complicity or commiseration. 'We struggle against these athletic Americans,' he said. 'It is hopeless. But we put up a brave fight.' Peter Danforth and Martha had returned to their places, impatient to resume the massacres. 'Are you sure you do not want to pet her?'

I dragged my gaze from Martha's legs to the hideous creature. 'I have an aversion to creepy crawlies.'

Laszlo shrugged and deposited the mantis (with some difficulty, since it clung to his hairy forearm) on the other side of the court netting. 'The name is Blathy. I come from Budapest. Monona is exact middle of No Place. So we must have a drink. After all, we are countrymen.'

'Uh – I don't think so.'

'*Yes*, Mr Loyner.' He leaned in close, till I could taste his sweat and a fetor of garlic. 'We belong to that great nation called 'Not America'.'

The two games resumed in parallel and Not America got thrashed in both.

We parted company under the floodlights.

2

The semester began in earnest and I devoted myself to teaching. At the end of a class, I would look for Martha Lutz in the faculty staff room. We met sometimes for lunch and, once, for dinner, where I failed to dim the light of appetite in my eyes. But my gorgeous colleague was elusive: I could make no sense of her signals.

One evening, returning from the faculty, I encountered the Hungarian again. He smiled, waving from the bookstore across Main Street, and I was surprised to find myself waving back. We ambled through town discussing our uprooted existences. Laszlo talked rapidly, with a strong accent and quirks of translation that caused him little embarrassment. 'Please,' he said, 'you must correct my use of your English.'

'Oh, mine is very much a minority dialect these days.'

We walked along the footbridge that spans the Ottumwa River. Bats were flitting between the opalescent orbs that illuminated either bank. A few shreds of cloud retained their glow in the dark chocolate sky, and the moon above steel rooftops was bloated and yellow. 'Tell me,' said Laszlo, 'why do not you join Peter and me at Lake Munro on Saturday? It is a reservoir. People go during migration to watch red tails.'

'That's a kind of fish, is it?'

'It is a hawk.'

There were, on my part at least, plans to lunch with Martha. When it transpired that she was already engaged (to whom? Doing what?), I found myself birding for the first time in my life.

Peter Danforth's Honda veered north, parallel with the weak brown river, and we mounted a ridge above the floodplain to see the gleaming sugar cubes and mock cathedrals of the university.

'Monona,' said Peter, 'is a bit of an oasis. A liberal island in a conservative sea.'

The highway became a bridge and the sheet metal of a lake was unveiled beneath us, framed by machine-cut sandstone cliffs. Along the northern shore there had grown up tangled woodland and, in a clearing beneath untutored trees, fat cars awaited their owners. We parked on the side of the road and walked – with foldable chairs and flasks and binoculars – a hundred yards or so to a bluff above the reservoir.

I had been issued with a pair of binoculars. What was I looking for?

'Heron,' said Peter.

'Heron,' said Laszlo.

'Where?'

'To your right,' said Laszlo.

'By the log,' said Peter. 'You ever heard one bark?'

'I have.'

'Which log?'

'When startled,' said Laszlo.

'Ooh,' said Peter.

'No, it is harrier. Look for white rump patch.' Laszlo's hand fastened on my elbow and steered me to deep blue sky. 'Up,' he said. 'Those black hanging birds are turkey vultures.'

These observations continued for half an hour. My arms grew weary from holding the binoculars and I began to kick at the dry soil. There was brief excitement at the antics of an osprey as it swept above the lake, flipped and dived unsuccessfully for a fish.

'You feel it now?' said Laszlo.

'What?'

'The drill.'

'Huh?'

'The drill of waiting and then – *pam* – winged beauty passes.'

We unfolded the chairs and sat, drinking sweet coffee and munching power bars. Lake Munro had been created under FDR, 'the one indisputably great President of the twentieth century,' according to Peter Danforth. Laszlo chewed and made an equivocal buzzing sound. 'Oh come *on*,' said Peter. 'You're not going to disagree.'

'I agree,' said Laszlo, 'about the New Deal…'

'And union rights, and some rudiments of welfare. And conservation efforts after the Dust Bowl.'

'True, true.'

'He was hated as much by business then as Bush is loved by business now…' Laszlo listened, wound the foil of his power bar into a tight ball and inserted it into his jacket pocket. Then he said one word: 'Yalta.'

Peter looked at him in dismay. 'Oh,' he said, 'that is low.'

'It was,' said Laszlo.

'The man was dying.'

'So why should we pay for it?'

'I grant, from an east European perspective —'

'Hungary,' said Laszlo, 'is not east. Nor is Bohemia or Poland. East is Belarus.'

Though reprimanded, Peter could not leave off politics. With his fingers joined in a spire of emphasis, he told us about the recent speech of a Democratic Primary candidate in a university playing field: the localised enthusiasm of a few hundred students, bashing plastic sticks together and whooping, against the utter indifference of hundreds more who flip-flopped or sneakered past without sparing more than a glance at the silver-haired senator who might become their President.

I went to pee in the bushes and, when I returned, the conversation had shifted a little.

'Let me tell you,' said Laszlo, slowly caressing his stubble. 'Burmese professor, when he came to Monona, the most remarkable thing — no soldiers in the street. Never a knock on the door at night or need for papers.' He flung out his arms. 'This — you know — is freedom.'

'You could say the same about *Belgium*. Only you wouldn't because there it's taken for granted.'

'America has always been a refuge.'

'To robber barons.'

'A country where the hobo can become President.'

'If he can raise a billion dollars.'

Laszlo puffed, grinned and got to his feet. No amount of liberal carping would shake his faith in the bastion and guarantor of liberty. 'I agree,' he said, patting Peter's shoulder, 'there is a lot of craziness. But this is still, at bottom, a sane society.'

On the way back to the car, my hosts stopped to inspect some yellow flowers. 'Goldenrod?' wondered Peter.

'Goldenrod,' said Laszlo. 'And this is big bluestem.'

'Prairie plants,' said Peter. His stare was heavy with

pedagogic intent. 'There was a time when a man could sit on his horse and barely see above the grasses.'

'Can you imagine,' asked Laszlo, and I made a game pretence of pretending to try.

'The first farmers had to plough through ten metres of peat and grass roots. The noise,' said Peter, 'was like pistol shots.'

'It was a perfect ecosystem. But not to European eyes.'

For much of the drive home, the entomologist addressed the back of my head. 'This is, you know, one of the most altered states in America. I speak ecologically. I am student of remnant prairie. What we called postage stamp – twelve acres between soy and corn.'

'Is it interesting work?'

'Oh my dear! I have discovered a new invertebrate. Subspecies I am certain of prairie mole cricket.' Fidgety with excitement, his English slipshod with it, Laszlo thumped my headrest. 'Unknown to science! Can you imagine the exitment?'

'Excitement,' corrected Peter kindly. 'What you feel, my friend, is excitement…'

3

Excitement of a different kind was what I hoped for. Martha Lutz began flirting with me. She glanced through the window as I bored a class of sophomores; she left post-it notes, like crumbs of sexual comfort, on the desk in my office inviting me to join her at the pictures or for dinner in town. We managed to skate around uncomfortable subjects (the war in Iraq was six months old and very far away) and this was inflaming evidence that she was as concerned as I was not to dampen the erotic charge. One evening, walking back from a college production of *The Cherry Orchard*, she took my arm and kissed me on the cheek. I nuzzled for more but all I got was a sample of earlobe and the cute, galling pressure of her fists in my chest as she eased me away.

Peter Danforth teased me about my infatuation. One night, invited to dinner by his gentle, svelte and heavily pregnant wife, I was warned about the temptress and her politics. 'But she's your friend,' I protested.

'So far as it goes,' said Peter. Kristen offered a satirical, nasal sough. 'Martha is on the dark side.'

'Different strokes,' I said, 'for different folks.'

'Hers are from Nebraska. They'd vote for a pig in a poke if it was a conservative.'

I shrugged and took a second serving of Kristen's risotto. Peter sent his hand across the table. 'She's part of the vanguard, John. And what makes it worse, she's articulate.'

'Don't,' said Kristen softly.

'Have you heard of a man called Harlan Boyd?'

'Peter…'

'I can discuss this in my own home!' His tone was sharp: it shook me from my digestive torpor.

'John *likes* her,' said Kristen.

'I'm not talking about Martha.'

'You're going to.'

'Harlan Boyd is a rich industrialist. And I mean rich: he more or less put our governor in office. He's in extraction, the Appalachians mostly. But now he's turning his attention to his home state. They've found bauxite. Right here in Panora County. Some of it in land the university owns.'

'So?'

'Harlan Boyd is a devout Baptist, and he's dangling this carrot in front of the university's face. Big bucks: an endowment for 'Christian Learning'. In return, he wants access to the bauxite.'

'Which is in university land.'

'Including Laszlo's swatch of prairie.'

'Are you sure,' I asked. 'He never said anything.'

'He's only known for about a week.'

'What does any of this have to do with Martha?'

'She worked for Harlan Boyd Extractions. She used to

advise them. For all I know, she still does.'

'Peter, she *is* an economist.'

'Harlan Boyd doesn't go about his work in a small way. In the Black Hills of South Dakota they're ripping the tops off mountains. For bauxite, they'll come with dumper trucks and strip-mine Laszlo's prairie into a little piece of the moon.'

Perhaps Peter was looking to me for an ally, but the truth is I'm no tree hugger. Though I meant mountains no harm, I considered myself a pragmatist and was not about to lose interest in Martha on account of her business dealings. Then, a few days later – perhaps to escape his worries – Laszlo telephoned me to suggest a second birding trip.

There was no danger of my becoming an outdoorsman: I went because I enjoyed Laszlo's company and curious parlance. He seemed to me a winning combination of the congenial and the ridiculous. As we walked, he talked entertainingly about his former life in Hungary: the garrulous ex-wife who turned to him for comfort each time a boyfriend left her, his deaf and cantankerous parents in their Budapest apartment overrun by malodorous cats. I wondered whether I should broach the topic of his threatened prairie, but Laszlo began extolling the beauties of Johnson Park: a grove of giant oaks with covered areas for benches and tables and, dotted about the wood, municipal barbecues like concrete lecterns. There was a gentle slope towards the glinting promise of a lake with a swathe of grassland beyond.

We sat on a bench above the view and began our vigil. 'Look,' said Laszlo. Tiny specks in the blue sky flashed of a sudden white, and we craned our necks to watch the slow passage of pelicans. Laszlo turned my attention to the flitting of a small yellow bird in some bushes.

'How do you know it's a yellow warbler?'

'Because that's what it is.' Laszlo cleared his throat. 'Werry curious bird, the yellow warbler. He is host species. You know what that means?'

'Uh, they raise other birds. Like with cuckoos.'

'Oh my dear, you are learning! The brown-headed cowbird lays his egg in the warbler's nest. And sometimes the alien egg is accepted, sometimes he is not. When there are many warbler eggs, the cowbird chick gets food. But when the eggs are few… guess what happen.'

'Uh – they eat it?'

'*Eat* the chick? What, are you crazy? Tinny little warblers?'

'Well I don't know.'

'Guess.'

'They chuck it out?'

Laszlo clicked his fingers with triumph. 'They don't throw out the impostor. They build around him. The female warbler makes a new nest above the first one. All season this can go on. The nest gets bigger and bigger. And each abandoned layer holds a cowbird egg.'

'Hatched?'

'Dead, John. Quite dead.'

The bird, its ears burning, flew off to join its migrating siblings and we watched the world drift towards evening. 'You have heard,' said Laszlo, 'about my prairie?'

'I have.'

'It is horrible!'

'But surely, if the site is so valuable – I mean biologically – they can't just develop it?'

'Dewelop!' Laszlo gave his throat a rasping scratch. 'This tinny bit of land I have studied for two years. Every centimetre I know and now… I ask for university support. But there is obvious convict of interest. So far I have heard *squit*.'

High in the oaks a cicada attempted to play, but its instrument was worn and blunt and the screed dwindled to silence.

'Once,' said Laszlo, 'the grassland of this state supported elk and bison. Now they survive only in the mountains. Sent back to refugia.'

'To what?'

Laszlo explained how, over millennia, the Black Hills of

South Dakota, or the Sweet Grass Hills of Montana, have been places of refuge from glaciations or droughts: islands among the ice sheets, oases above the desert. He sucked in his breath. 'You know what a man said to me? At a party in college he said: "I don't believe in global warming. And besides, we will be able to cope with it."' The laugh that followed was a bark. Then Laszlo snuffed and rubbed the fleshy tip of his nose and invited me to lead the way back to civilisation.

4

A fortnight passed and my friendship with the Danforths deepened, even as Martha Lutz toyed with my advances. Students tramped dutifully into and out of my classes without betraying enthusiasm for their studies or their tutor. I feared I was having little impact and said as much over beer on the Danforth stoop; whereupon Kristen, taking pity on a lonely and undersexed Englishman, invited me to join them on a visit to her parents in Minneapolis.

Wanting Martha to sample neglect, I accepted.

The year had turned – it was early October – and the cornfields with their belts of aspen were tawny coloured. I dozed in the car, lifting fitfully the cowl of an eyelid to find the landscape unchanged: the planted grids, silos, and farmhouses sitting out the endless siege of the plains. When Kristen slept, Peter at the wheel talked politics.

'It's like McCarthy all over again. We're so terrified of terrorists we don't notice those in our midst.' Seeing my expression in the mirror, he told me about witch-hunts in universities, the power of conservative talk-show hosts and the servility of the media. It was a long day's drive to the Twin Cities and we stopped three times at roadside diners. Each time Kristen went to the bathroom, Peter would resume his lamentations. There festered within him the terrible bitterness of American radicals: pushed back, like one of Laszlo's endangered crickets, to their last redoubt in academia. Even there they were losing ground, harried by zealots of the right, by corporate interests. 'It astonishes me,' said Peter, unaware that his wife was coming up behind him, 'that people are *voting* for this poison. Against their interests.'

'Maybe,' said Kristen, 'because this poison doesn't tell them they're assholes.'

We swept north through Iowa: the vanished empire of grass. By nightfall we were in Minneapolis. We pulled up outside a white wooden house in the suburbs and were greeted by Kristen's parents. Mr Dymling was a retired, small press publisher; his wife was still teaching English at high school. They offered us a light supper and, seeing how tired I was, held back from friendly interrogation. Theirs was the frank, unfussy hospitality for which Americans are famous. I was not to expect entertainment but was invited to settle into the even tempo of their household.

The following days were taken up with kitchen chats and gardening, with sumptuous meals and bloated strolls about a nearby lake. On our last day, we youngsters went into town and explored a sculpture park. We stopped, at literary Kristen's insistence, on a bland highway bridge above the Mississippi, from which some famous poet had thrown himself years ago.

'Boy,' said Peter, contemplating the far-below river. 'To plunge from this height – with all the time it gives you to relent. That's more than a death wish. There's real punishment in it.'

The next day we left early for Monona. We made good speed and reached the town by nightfall. A copy of the local newspaper had been stuffed into the letterbox of my apartment.

MONONA SCIENTIST ARRESTED

I gulped at the photograph of Laszlo Blathy chained to a bulldozer. "A college lecturer took direct action today in protest against…" was all that I read before I ran out the door and chased the Danforths' car down the street.

Kristen lowered her window. 'Look at this,' I said. With our heads intimately bowed, we read the front page.

★

Within a few days, the incident was arousing statewide – then national – news interest. Laszlo was much pursued, and camera crews loitered outside the biology building even as Boyd Extractions were stripping the land a few hundred yards from the disputed prairie.

'He's got balls,' I said, 'you have to admit. We didn't expect it of him.'

Peter was less impressed. 'Having balls,' he said, 'only gives them a target to aim at.'

Laszlo, in his battle against the prairie's destruction, welcomed his newfound notoriety. When America's biggest cable news network approached him for an interview, Peter attempted to dissuade him. 'You gotta be careful with these people. They won't be on your side.'

But Laszlo was cocksure, fired up with an activist's hope. The media attention would, he felt certain, shame the university into protecting his mole cricket.

'Please, listen to good advice. The network is your enemy.'

'I will persuade them.'

'Have you not *seen* how they operate?'

'I do not like to watch television. It is so enerwating.'

'That's precisely why you should keep away.'

In his dogged way, Laszlo would not be dissuaded. 'But you know,' he said, 'I do like to watch old mooies.'

'Old what?'

'Old American mooies. Humphrey Beaucart. Whoreson Wellace.'

'Jesus,' said Peter as we left the biology building. 'There's nothing we can do to stop it.'

'Maybe you should trust him.'

Peter stopped and looked at me reproachfully. 'I trust Laszlo. It's my country I have no faith in.'

5

Martha came to find me on the day of the TV interview. It was the first time she had been in my apartment and she affected obliviousness to its disorder. Her long suede skirt parted in a longitudinal smile to reveal, as she sat, a leg in white silk stockings. 'I've missed your company,' she said.

'Well I missed yours. Though I'm sure you didn't pine too badly.'

I did not sit down but travelled between my lounge and my kitchen, finding hospitable excuses – coffee, milk and sugar – not to settle. Martha moistened her carmine lips. 'Why are you looking at your watch?'

'God, am I?'

'You have work to do. You mustn't let me keep you from your Entropy Theory of Affluence.' Mention of my PhD was always meant to tease. Martha did not believe in the finitude of profit.

'Sorry,' I said, 'it's just that Laszlo's speaking in an hour and I'm nervous for him.'

Martha lowered her eyelids; they were glazed with jade iridescence, the lashes clotted with mascara. I confessed that I was due at the Danforths' house, and she insisted on accompanying me.

Peter and Kristen bade us welcome. We gathered in their lounge and Kristen excused herself to fetch snacks from the kitchen. Peter was in a provocative mood. 'It's not normally a channel we watch,' he told Martha. 'But I guess for you, it's like taking orders from Moscow.' Then he too escaped – before a riposte could be assembled – to the sanctuary of the kitchen.

'Sheesh,' said Martha, flopping delectably on the sofa.

'They can be so self-righteous.'

'It's the tetchiness that comes of being in opposition,' I said.

From this conciliatory quip, I date the ruination of my hopes. I became embroiled in that forbidden, political argument. For weeks we had censored ourselves when it came to recent events, but Martha had been provoked and now, detecting fellow feeling, she launched on a tirade. There was, she said, no mistaking the secret pleasure that liberals took in their army's setbacks. They craved a quagmire in Iraq as much as conservatives an easy victory. A sentimental concern for those poor boys sent to die disguised a desire for bodybags, each one to contain a metaphorical piece of the hated President.

'There *are* reasons for disliking the man,' I said, and proceeded to list them. Martha was silent and tight-lipped. From the kitchen came the sound of corn popping. Did I really care enough to have this discussion? The vulgarity, the universal mendacity and silliness of politics have always seemed obvious to me. How can people surrender their intellect to a tribe, or campaign so passionately for a windbag you wouldn't want for a neighbour? This universal contempt had always served me well; yet now, in the comfort of the Danforth living room, the mild and placid certainty of the woman I so desired was driving me crazy.

'I know,' said Martha, 'why you people are angry.'

'You people?'

'The President is guided by his faith. I hear what you're saying about science and stuff. But human understanding is limited, John. I trust the President's instincts because there's nothing he does that he doesn't pray over. And that reassures me. It gives me *comfort*.'

I was still gaping when our hosts returned, bearing popcorn and a tray of coffees. Peter turned on the TV and flipped through a dozen channels before we reached the garish bridge of a news mothership. A stout, scowling man with a sports commentator's jaw and an abundance of pomaded hair was plugging his forthcoming show. "I'll be asking if these so-called *professors* are using their influence to corrupt our kids. Freedom of speech, or propaganda for terrorists? Join me, Bill Kerber, on *Those Who Hate America*, in half an hour on –"

'John,' said Martha, patting the sofa beside her perfect ass, 'won't you sit down?'

'I'm too nervous. There he is, look.'

Porno-glow lettering swooped across the screen to the accompaniment of flatulent brasses; now, looking pale and apprehensive, half a size too small for Peter Danforth's suit, Laszlo Blathy clung to the news desk while his interrogator raised a manly eyebrow. The music reached a crescendo, dissolved, and above the newscaster's shoulder a picture of a common cricket appeared with the tagline: *Jobs or Bugs?*

"Welcome back, I'm Denton Brome. My guest now in the studio is an entomologist. In plain English that means he studies *critters* – the bugs you and I squish beneath our shoes. Three days ago, on a patch of land outside the University of Monona, Iowa, Dr Lazelow Blatty chained himself to the fender of an earthmover. He wanted to save what he calls a 'precious patch of prairie' from commercial development. Fifty jobs – in a depressed rural state – depend on the project, but Dr Blatty insists the *bug* he's been studying must be protected at all cost... So, Dr Blatty..."

The picture switched to a sweating, blinking Laszlo. 'Oh,' groaned Peter. 'He looks like Mr Magoo.'

"... You chained yourself to machinery. Is that responsible behaviour for a man in your profession?"

"Well," said Laszlo, "I was running out of alternatives."

"How long did it take the authorities to cut you loose? It says here three hours."

"It was a strong chain."

"I'll say. We have pictures..." Now the network screened press photographs: not the ones his friends had seen in *The Monona Watchtower* of Laszlo serene, his arms raised like an early Christian martyr while the headless torsos of officialdom stood about debating how to counter his resistance, but later shots of the operation to break his chains (Laszlo frozen in a grimace while the blowtorch flared) and what followed, as with absurd and theatrical sombreness three police officers pressed the dangerous felon into a police car. "There you are," said Denton Brome, "being taken into custody." Laszlo seemed not to know that the camera was on him and continued to scowl myopically at the monitor in the desk. "How much did it cost taxpayers to have you blowtorched from the machinery?"

"That is not the point. In America, direct protesting…"

"I believe you're a guest in this country. Isn't that right? You're not a citizen."

"I am Lecturer in Entomology at University of Monona…"

"Let me see if I can get this straight: you monopolize the county police for an entire afternoon with your antics – just to save a few bugs *I've* never heard of – and you're a guest of the United States."

"Can I…?"

"Which has received you warmly."

"Can I tell…?"

"And rewarded you with a prestigious job."

"… about the cricket?"

"Tell us about the cricket."

Laszlo took a deep breath. "First of all," he said, "he is werry rare cricket. His habitat is also werry rare. In 1850, prairie covered most of State of Iowa. Today there is hardly any. This is the most altered state – ecologically speaking – in all America…"

"Grows good corn, though."

"Uh… Wiewers will no doubt be familiar with mole cricket – *Gryllotalpa gryllotalpa* – that lives underground. Mole cricket has number of subspecies. It is fascinating opportunity to study evolutionary process."

"Can you get to a point?"

"This *is* the point. What I have found is a new subspecies of prairie mole cricket. It is distinguished by uncommonly large tympanum, much more typical in field species. It is werry tinny but equipped with strong forelegs which it uses for borrowing…"

"This is all very interesting, Doctor Blatty. Do you think a family going hungry for want of jobs really cares about some bug they can't even see?"

"We cannot permit species to go extinct."

"I'm sure there are plenty other places where it lives happily — munching grass or whatever it does."

"But… no, but…"

"The fact is no one seems too concerned about a bug's welfare except for you. Do you feel very isolated?"

"It is *surviwal* what I am talking about!"

"When you get up off your knees and stop playing with your microscope, do you ever think about the people involved in this and what *they* need to survive?"

"This is unique subspecies. It is to my knowing everywhere else… uh… impossible to find."

"You could probably get a big fat grant, though, to look for it."

"Big fat…?"

"There's the perfect compromise. You get your study money and the good honest folk of Panora County get to feed and clothe their kids."

"But it may not occur elsewhere. All I am asking is for Boyd Extractions to rewise their dewelopment plan. Lots of space exists in agricultural use. Why destroy this prairie?"

"Well, Dr Blatty, you'll have to take it up with them. Maybe you could chain yourself to their head office, or bury your feet in concrete outside the CEO's drive. It's amazing you people manage to find time for these gestures. Most of us are too busy putting food on the table."

"What? What!"

Already the interview was over. Laszlo lost his place on the screen and we were treated to a close up of Denton Brome. "After the break," he said, his head tipping with emphasis, "we'll be heading to California and its devastating forest fires. An incendiary new study asks – are environmentalists to blame?" Garish lettering slammed across Broam's face and we returned to the bluster and bromides of commercials.

'For God's sake,' I heard myself shout, 'turn it off!'

Peter obliged and we sat listening to the silence. I heard Kristen get up to go to the bathroom. Martha looked glumly at her coffee cup.

I pushed through the wire mesh to the yard. A minute or two later, Peter joined me. 'Martha's gone home,' he said, eyeing me carefully. I wondered when Laszlo would return. All of Monona, for want of better entertainment, would have watched the interview. What could we, what could anyone, say to console him?

6

In the end I spoke to Laszlo only once. It was on the corner of Jefferson and Main, where I had gone, back bent against the wind, to pay my respects to the ATM machine. I saw him, wrapped in a scarf and gabardine, leaving the Blue Bison restaurant. I froze with indecision until he saw me and jaywalked across the street.

'Laszlo, I've been –'

'Busy.'

'All the same, I want to say how sorry I am.'

'Ah my dear, what can you do?' He seemed to glance, a little pained as though from wind, across my shoulder.

'Have you time for a drink?'

'I must be packing.'

'Packing?'

Laszlo shrugged – a gesture that seemed to involve his whole body. I contemplated his upturned, philosophical palms.

'I don't suppose the last few days have been much fun.'

'Fun, no.' Laszlo smiled wanly. 'You remember the cowbird?'

'The what?'

'The yellow warbler and the cowbird egg.'

I searched the dormant recesses of my brain. Laszlo watched me feign remembrance.

'It is,' he said, 'the same for me. I embarrass everyone. Republican, Democrat. They want to be ignoring. So they build a wall around me. Like the yellow warbler with the cowbird's egg. You have no idea what I am talking about, have you? It does not matter. They were going to make cuts anyhow. This way I get *glowing* references.'

And so we parted: two Not Americans who would leave few traces in the New World. Only with Martha Lutz had I made an impression. As I threw myself into my paper for the end of semester symposium, she began to pursue me openly. Invitations to the cultural offerings of college arrived thick and fast. She suggested a weekend trip to Chicago. At each advance I measured in myself the absence of desire. I had come to America hungry, aching for who knows what fulfilment. Being unoriginal, I assumed the ache was erotic. But I had spoiled those chances by acknowledging what divided us. Doing so had changed nothing – except that I had lost my appetite.

The Ghost Who Bled

THERE WAS NO CRYING at my funeral and I was glad of it. It made me proud to see how bravely my mother bade farewell to her youngest boy. My sister, Ayaka, touched her elbow in case she faltered but my mother stood firm throughout the ceremony. She knew that my death was honourable, that I embraced it with tears of joy.

I was sad, of course, to be leaving this life. Sometimes it had been very sweet to me. Like that time I kissed Eriko in the cherry orchard behind her father's house. Or when my older brother came home in his soldier's uniform, with a flag furled and tucked under his arm, and everyone in the village came over to listen to his stories of our glorious deeds in Manchukuo. But there was no point regretting my death. It was, after all, impossible to undo.

I was gone already when the mouth of hell opened thirty miles away. A hundred thousand brilliant souls fled before the darkness. They tore silently, like reflections of sun from a giant mirror, across the sky above our village. Trees shook, flags shivered, in a premonitory gust of wind. The whole earth lurched, as though woken from ancient dreams. My mother may have thanked the gods that I had gone ahead of this terrible storm and its aftermath of corpse shadows, powdered stone and mangled iron, the archipelagos of scorched flesh on the backs of survivors.

But I would see them. I would stand on a hillside and gaze down, with these dead man's eyes, at the evaporated city. And long before that day, at the moment of catastrophe, following so close to my own, I felt the air quiver, I heard the strange thunder. Hiding in my cave beside the beach near our village, I watched the sideways ripples on the sea – the cross-stitching of old waves and new, like the conflict between two moons. I thought the world was ending. I hoped it might, to eradicate the incomprehensible truth: that I was still conscious.

After the shockwaves, after the great cloud and its contrails like scars in the sky's belly, I hobbled back to the village where I had lived and cowered beneath my beloved's house. I listened to the shuffling of sandaled feet above my head and to the mournful drone of her father's voice. Sometimes her mother replied, very quietly, like a cat moaning in a bad dream. But Eriko was completely silent. Down in the sand, keeping company with crickets and sand fleas, I strained to hear my sweetheart's voice, longing in vain to hear her weep. Eventually I had to move. I was being tortured by hunger. I could not rid myself of old habits.

The next few days I spent in the cave beside the sea. When the beach was empty I would take a walk along the shoreline, looking at the flotsam – mainly pieces of wood, a few barnacled crates, dead crabs, a GI's boot, a charred hand. I thought about my corpse, how it should be floating somewhere out in that immensity, or trapped on the ocean bed, swirling with hungry fish.

Some course of action had to be followed. But I was powerless to make a decision. I seemed to have left my will in the fuselage, or else it had left me long ago, well before my death, when I was still a boy perhaps, out catching squid in the sea at night, or devoting myself to lessons at school. The entire world, from which I could not divorce myself, seemed to float on indecision.

Then the second bomb fell.

A few villagers stirred from their houses after the shrill, whining and divine voice had finished sounding on the radio. Who could believe what had happened? Several people I had known halted and seemed to peer in my direction. A few of them narrowed their faces, as though confronted by the smell of something rotten. But it was impossible: everyone knew what had become of me.

Resting in a moonlit wood, I remembered that night a picture from when I was little. It came from an old scroll, the *Gaki Zoshi*. My mother had shown it to me one afternoon while the cherry blossom snowed down outside our house. The scroll showed a group of hideous ghosts crawling among the living. The ghosts had been gluttons in their lifetimes, they had loved worldly things too much and now they could not tear themselves away. After my mother showed me this picture in her book, I could not sleep for many nights. I was terrified that one of the hungry ghosts — with its staring eyes and gaping mouth and bloated scaly belly — was squatting beside me in the darkness. When I told my mother about these fears, she said that ghosts were harmless; we could not see them, or touch them, or hear them. Even when they sat beside us, we knew nothing about it. And so, having attended my own obsequies, I had to face the truth. I was dead, of course. I had no right to hang on among the living.

To my eternal shame, I did. I longed to reveal myself to Ayaka, or to find Eriko where she slept and weep into her shoulder. Unwilling to leave familiar surroundings, I fashioned a rod; I made a line from the bark of a *shuro* palm and twisted thorns to make a hook. I fished in the cove at night. In the early hours, when the fishermen were out at sea, I would steal fruit from their gardens.

One day in September, when my solitude became unendurable, a suffocating weight, I ran through the desolate street and returned to my mother's house, to *my* house, where I had spent the whole of my life and to which my soul was most deeply attached. Trembling with apprehension, I stalked up and down in the grove. There was a single faint light in the house. I could visualise every detail of the lampshade with its pattern of red cherries and the simpler earthenware vase into which, months before, I had fixed a candlestick to replace the useless light bulb.

Night fell. An obscure bird called loudly above my head. Ayaka, I knew, would be out with the women, mending nets. I summoned all my nerve, or what I still imagined was my nerve, and crept up the familiar wooden steps.

My mother was kneeling on the floor, mending a gown with some wrong-coloured string. Her back was turned. I could tell that she sensed me. I saw her fingers stop moving and her body grow rigid. Did my presence make her hair stand on end? I could have spent eternity in that familiar room, with my mother kneeling as though at prayer, sensing her son and resisting her senses. I knew she would not turn, and that I could no more speak to her than fish may breathe out of water. But my death had not released me from time: I knew that I was transgressing, that Ayaka would soon return. I looked about the darkening room with only the feeble light from the candle to see by. And to my consternation, I could see no pictures of myself. The school photograph of me in my cadet uniform had given way to a pale rectangular ghost, a frame-shaped absence on the wall. And where were my schoolbooks? Gone, or sold, or used up as kindling. Mother, I wanted to cry, where are my clothes that you used to fold so lovingly? In my frenzy I must have made a noise, shaking cabinets and opening doors. Yet my mother, whom I could discern immobile in the deepening gloom, did not speak or move. Her face was averted, her eyes fixed on a spot on the floor.

Shivering with grief, I fled to the grove at the back of our garden where, after a long time, I looked up to behold a white figure on the porch of the house. The figure withdrew and I advanced to discover some green tea and plums left on a dish beside the pond. It was an offering to the dead. I took it. But my shame the next day was so great, so terrible – like the aftermath of rotten fish on a man's stomach – that I fled the garden, and the village, and the district, to begin my lonely wanderings.

★

Our prefecture of Yamaguchi had not suffered so much as its northern neighbour. I found out what had happened there; being dead could not spare me the worst of it. I heard the feeble croaking of survivors in their makeshift hospital tents. I saw a scorched parchment of flattened houses and fallen trees, becoming at the centre a sort of nothingness, white like an ulcer, or a quarry exhausted by industry. Close to the centre, I heard a doctor say, the sand had turned to glass.

I could not stay in that valley. It was too full of ghosts. There was no mistaking their distended bellies, the scaly and corrupted flesh, the eyes dulled by shame and despair. Living people – doctors and orderlies, stinking foreign devils with faces so reproachably alive – walked among the corpses. They may have thought they were helping. But there is no remedy for broken spirits.

How did I know they were ghosts? Because some of them *saw* me. A few weary eyes met mine, one or two heads faintly nodded. Others even spoke to me. I could not tell what they were saying. Perhaps they wished to know my story, or to tell me their own. I could have listened more closely. But it would have been to scoop ashes into my mouth.

I pressed on, following the coast, through the decay of autumn. The hills around Kure were being stripped for firewood. I slept under a mound of leaves and sawdust in a newly hacked clearing and nearly yapped with fright when a voice behind me said, 'You'll catch your death out here, friend.' I beheld a scrawny, dishevelled creature, dressed in the tatters of a soldier's uniform. His face was thickly bearded and his cheeks hung like empty pouches where the fat used to be. 'I've found an old shrine beside a stream,' he said. 'We can shelter there from the wind. Don't be afraid, I mean no harm. My name is Honest Morito.' He reached down and squeezed my shoulder. It was the first time anyone had touched me since my death. 'Listen,' he said, 'I'm travelling north to the place where I used to live. It's a little village in the hills near Okayama. Come on, the night will soon be upon us and someone might steal our shelter…'

Honest Morito tried hard to deserve his name. He was a jolly and talkative ghost; he never pushed me to speak about my life but assumed that I had lived it well. He showed me such respect on our difficult road that I almost believed in my honour again. 'I hope to be reborn,' I said one night as we huddled beside a dying fire. 'That's why I'm going north.'

'A strange way of putting it. I just want to pick up my old life.'

I said nothing, feeling only pity for him. How could he hope to regain himself, or stay honest, when he was a shadow blown about the world?

After the snow began to fall, Honest Morito betrayed his name. He stole, with my help, the scrawny rooster from a dung heap. We broke into rice stores and ran, trembling with cold and fear, into ditches to chew our loot. Sometimes I woke up to find him praying. Do the gods hear the dead? I doubt it very much. Yet perhaps they had taken pity on him, I thought one morning, to explain his absence from my side. In the next village I heard rumours that a poor farmer had been robbed and murdered during the night. Nobody could believe a neighbour was responsible. Search parties set out to find the culprit. Only I knew that they would never catch him. Honest Morito had disappeared straight to Hell.

As for me, my hope of rebirth was only a dream. Instead I learned, with the cunning of necessity, how to inhabit another man's body. In the four years that followed, I was a fisherman in Kobe, then a gardener in Kyoto. He was a quiet young man, that gardener, who knew little about plants but worked hard to please his employers. He had few friends. Women barely noticed him. He seemed to prefer solitude and liked to sit in the calm of a Zen garden, watching with empty thoughts the stilled flow of sand, the nodding of cherry boughs. Yes, I could have stayed in that man forever. But there lived in one of the gardens a very old monk. He worshipped in a small temple and kept watch on the progress of the seasons from his wooden bench under a bamboo screen. The first time he saw the gardener I felt uneasy. I was afraid of his placid, wrinkled smile and distrusted the monk's vigilance. When, after many months, he extended a bony arm and waved us over, I could not turn away.

The old monk said nothing. Calmly he scrutinised the gardener's face. I wanted to run. The monk tilted his pale head, as though trying to look *past* the gardener – or through him, into *my* eyes. I sensed him probing for me. He began to speak, addressing my host, about the rain and the problems of frost. Outwardly, he was just an old monk talking to a gardener. Inwardly, he was trying to prize me out of my shell. I knew that my presence had been detected. 'You should rest,' the old monk said. 'You have laboured much and needlessly.' The gardener thanked the monk but refused the offer of a place on his bench. Bowing with respect, he returned to his flowerbed.

In the morning I fled Kyoto.

★

The last man I inhabited was a factory worker in Wakayama. I did not enjoy life on the workshop floor, where we fixed dials on wireless radios, and soon I was longing to see my village again, to swim in the cove and sleep beneath its wind-twisted pines. Like the ghosts in the *Gaki Zoshi*, I have loved the world too much. Or to be precise, I have loved *my* world – the sufficient planet of home. It was no easy decision to shed my disguise. I feared the long journey south and dreaded what I might find there. Desire, however, proved stronger than fear.

Five years dead, I returned to my village.

My mother's house was sinking into the undergrowth. Weeds pushed their way up the wooden steps. Everything was in darkness. The obvious thing to do was to ask a neighbour what had happened. But that was quite impossible, of course, and anyway, I did not need to be told. My mother was gone.

Ayaka I found by the fish-gutting sheds, washing linen in the stream. She did not see me where I hid behind a pile of stinking crates. I recognised a man's clothes spread out to dry in the morning sun. Their owner revealed himself soon enough.

Yoshi had always admired my sister. Should I have lived to protect her from such a fool? Had I betrayed her by my sacrifice? Foul, stinking Yoshi had climbed into her belly to be sure of his claim. I cannot believe that she willingly accepted his marriage proposal. With mother dead and brothers killed, an orphan, what choice did my sister have?

I crawled away, hollow with impotent rage, and bedded down on the edge of old Nagayama's farm. In the morning I awoke to hear children's voices on the other side of the barn door. I was dazzled by morning sunlight. Above the shield of my arm, I saw a small boy and a small girl gaping at me. The boy was carrying a basket of white mushrooms. It fell from his grip, pale soft skulls rolling in the grass. I tried to speak, to reassure them, but what emerged from my parched throat sounded like a growl.

The children were new to the world. They did not know not to see me. I blocked my ears and considered hitting them to make their screaming stop. I chased them from the barn door, only to behold a fat young man running from old Nagayama's house, brandishing a rake. I could hear him bellowing as I ran through the orchard – and scalped myself on a washing line. Clothes fell onto the grass; the line wavered with a faint hum like a struck chord. Sprawling on the ground, I saw a young woman staring. I forgot at once my status. I hobbled on my knees and tried to catch her hands.

'Eriko.'

I noticed peasant clothes, tough material for working in the fields. She pulled her hands up to her chest. 'Children,' she cried, 'run and fetch your father!'

'Eriko, it's me. I've come back.'

Retreating, her face savage with fear, she turned her eyes from me. 'Hanazo! Hanazo!'

'Eriko! You *do* see me!'

For an instant, a little instant worth exchanging with all eternity, she looked at the place where I knelt. Then her eyes slid up to the rake travelling at speed through the morning mist. I managed to avoid the blow, falling onto my backside. Hanazo Kuwata swiped several times above my head, fanning me with the rake's fingers. We had been enemies at school. I knew him to be a coward and a bully: Hanazo the Monkey. To see Eriko take refuge behind him was unendurable. I shielded my eyes against it, and opened them long after the breeze from the rake had ceased. They were walking back to the house, the parents escorting their children to safety. I saw only Eriko's back, her hair bound up in a simple knot, the nape I had kissed.

For two days I scavenged and thieved. All my victims had known me once. Now, though I stole food in broad daylight, sometimes from the very table where they were eating breakfast, the villagers blushed and looked away. Imagine the license! Raised in obedience of the law, I now found that I could do whatever I pleased. I tripped up grim patriarchs in the street and urinated in my headmaster's fishpond. Shrieking and gibbering like a *Kabuki* ghost, I upset vegetable carts and spilled dumplings from their bowls. I scratched at the doors of frightened children, whose parents merely moved them to another room. This behaviour of mine continued, it worsened with every averted face, every back turned to my mischief. *Look at me*, I meant to say, *look at me, you bastards.* Until, one afternoon, somebody did.

The plums were too enticing to be left on the stall. I did not see the fruit seller, having decided to ignore those who ignored me. I raised the ripest plum to my mouth.

'Stop! Put that back at once!'

A round, narrow-eyed, piglike face loomed over mine. I had never seen it before. 'I'm warning you. If you don't pay for that, I'll smash your face.' From behind his back, like a conjuror, the stranger produced a walking stick. My heart skipped with terror and joy. I lowered the plum towards the stall. The fruit seller lowered his stick. I snatched the plum and bit into it.

'Thief! Stop him. Thief!'

Where did my energy come from, which allowed me to run so fast, while the fruit seller gave chase? Whoever this man was – a newcomer to the village – he was not as swift as me. Having shaken him off my tail, I hid in the dusty alley behind the post office. Slumping down, panting, with the plum bleeding in my hand, I noticed that I had cut my foot.

'Here, I've found him!'

Heaving for breath, his piggy eyes wide with triumph, the fruit seller pointed his stick at my head. I reached down to touch the gash on my foot. 'You left a trail,' he said. 'That's how I tracked you down.' I said nothing, only looked at my bloodied fingers. In my other hand I squeezed the wounded plum. 'Well, come on,' the fruit seller shouted. 'I've got him cornered.'

Two policemen appeared in the mouth of the alley. They peered over the stranger at the place where I sat. I knew them both. Yuichi used to spy on my sister from the grove at the bottom of our garden. I thumped him for it once, when the teacher had left the classroom. His colleague, Emon, had been three years below me at school, and I remembered the look of admiration he gave me on the day I volunteered. There was no such expression on his face now. The policemen shared a nervous glance. 'What are you waiting for?' demanded the fruit seller. 'Aren't you going to arrest him?'

Yuichi spoke first. Already he was reaching for the fruit seller's sleeve. 'Whom should we arrest?' he said. 'There's nobody here.'

The fruit seller gasped in bewilderment. 'This man… here… right in front of you.'

Emon shook his head. Yuichi transferred his grip from the man's sleeve to his arm. 'We'll pay for the fruit,' he said. Emon took the other arm and they wheeled him about. 'You must have imagined it.'

The last thing I saw of the fruit seller, he was casting his eyes down at his palm, in which a coin had been pressed, fresh from Emon's pocket. His piggy face was swollen with incomprehension. Nobody would blame him for his behaviour. He was new to the village and knew nothing about my story.

I was meant to fly to my glorious death on 6th August 1945. But the aeroplane was already scrap and failed to get airborne. Its godlike days were ended. So too my country's. We limped away, like dogs in disgrace, to hide in the shadows. Eventually my country emerged but I did not. There was no room in my village for a grounded thunder god. I should have killed myself, sitting in that silent cockpit, with the ruin of my world far gone like a wood blown naked by a winter storm. I should have plunged that sword into my belly and saved my honour. But after the disbelief and the rage, after the tears and the tantrum, with blood welling up beneath my headband where I had dashed my forehead against the controls, I was filled with the sweetness of living. I remembered Eriko's parted lips, and the cherry blossom, and the taste of cabbage soup as only my mother could make it.

I chose dishonour.

So it has been my punishment to walk as a shade in the brilliant world. I have been the scratching at a locked door, the tingle in a woman's spine, the fruit stolen from the shelf.

I am the ghost who bled.

The Soul Surgeons

WE CROSSED THE RIVER at Southwark, having learned at The
Rose the whereabouts of the scrivener. Harry Talbot was
leading, while Bull in the stern complained of a toothache that
made him grip his jaw with both hands. I promised him some
oil of cloves to ease the pain. 'If it continues,' I said, 'you will
have to have it pulled.' Thomas Bull, our Shoreditch Hercules,
turned pale at the thought and shook his head. He did not
suffer pain bravely.

'Faster,' said Talbot to the boatman. It was early May as I
recall, yet the sun was strong and kites wheeled above the city.
What carrion did they glimpse from their ocean of sky?

'That other,' I dared say, though a crease of irritation deep
as a scar formed between Talbot's eyes, 'is fortunate to be out
of town. Did he not write those lines? *We'll cut your throats, in
your temples praying.*' I quoted from the libel found in the Dutch
churchyard. It was the work of one 'Tamburlaine', who raged
against foreign merchants and against those in government
who profited from their protection.

Talbot eyed me unpleasantly. 'I did not have you for a
frequenter of the theatre.'

I assured him that I was not, that such places belonged
south of the river, among the whores and the bear pits.
'Anyway,' I said, 'which is it – Marlin or Morley?'

'It is slippery,' said Talbot. 'Like the man himself. But we
will find his friend.' The boat sighed into the sand and rocked.
Bull moaned behind his paws as we stepped out. 'He is a

playmaker, too. The one about mad Hieronymo. But of course *you* would not know it. You are a good, pious fellow.'

I was not such a fool as to miss the mockery in Talbot's voice. My superior in the service, he was tireless in reminding me of it. It had been to his hands that the directive came, straight from the Privy Council, to find out the author of those incitements to commotion.

We headed north, Harry Talbot stepping nimbly between porters and tradesmen, never spotting his boots in the drains. On Watling Street Bull knocked two beggars' heads together, and their complaints pursued us halfway to Cheapside.

'These playmakers,' said Talbot, 'inspire men to bloody violence. Did you not see, a few months back, *The Massacre at Paris*?'

Bull nodded and grinned. This must have chafed his rotten tooth, for he promptly clawed his cheek. 'Very cruel,' he said, 'and excellent.'

'A plague on poetasters. They promise more than the world delivers. Well, we must cut away at untruth.'

We waited at the sign of The Ram, by Bow Church, for evening to fall: drinking slowly, our minds adrift. We could see the scrivener's lodgings, even the window — ajar on account of the heat — behind which he sat, ignorant of his fate.

It was Bull's toothache that hastened things. After perhaps an hour of his muted groaning, Talbot pushed his tankard from him and complained: 'Cannot you bear it like a man?'

Bull, mighty Bull, quaked and sought my sympathy with his eyes. 'It is murder,' he said. 'Waiting so, I can think of nothing else.'

'Another's pain would distract you,' Talbot said, standing. He deserved authority over better men than us. A groat from his fist clattered on the table. 'We will go instantly, no more to hear your mammering.'

As we crossed the street, I endeavoured to soothe Bull's wounded pride. He would be less cruel at the question if his spirits were good. The landlord opened to us without question or protest; he knew Talbot's face from previous raids. On the creaking stairs the lodgings smelled of sweat and gruel and Billingsgate fish, not of the freshest. We devoured step after step. I felt something of a traitor, for there is a kinship in all professions, and like our quarry I was a scrivener. It was my task to document the cleansing of the city, to witness deepest sin and error and record the mystery, when at last it is revealed, of Our Saviour's mercy.

Bull pounded at the appointed door. It was dark in that stairway and we blinked at the light when, timidly, the occupant opened to us. He was promptly pinioned by Bull. A thin man, scraggy-bearded and pale, with ink-brindled fingers, the scrivener protested, cried for help, stared with bulging eyes when Bull covered his mouth.

'We have a warrant for your arrest,' said Talbot, after requesting a nod from the scrivener to confirm his identity. I cast an eye about the den and recognised its desolation from my own life as a student-servant, when I had often been hungry for a cue of bread. While Talbot brandished his letters of authority, I looked over the papers strewn about the scrivener's table. I glimpsed letters in divers hands, verses with blottings out, a fresh page with *dramatis personae* and the title *Cornelia* written upon it.

Harry Talbot joined me in the window-light. 'Go speak with him,' he said. 'He is so distempered that his feet may turn to water. And I do not mean to *carry* him to prison.'

I left Talbot at the table and went to kneel beside the scrivener. He was silent now, for fear of Bull's clammy hand, and sat on the floor embracing his knees. I did not meet his eyes but looked to the flagon of malmsey beside the bed. I offered him to drink but he refused; the flagon went instead to Bull, who drained it.

'Let him take some clothes,' I said. It was easier to address a prisoner indirectly. 'A cap and that mantle.'

'Where am I being taken?' the scrivener asked. His voice sounded calm enough; but he looked, as often they did, as though he had aged a decade since our interruption.

'Where you will need warm clothes,' I said.

'Have I time to write a letter?'

'That is not in my gift.'

Hereupon Talbot returned from the side room, his face afire with triumphant indignation, brandishing some handwritten pages. 'You were a fool not to burn these,' he said to the scrivener. 'You were a fool to set these things *down*. I am no doctor of theology but a God-fearing Christian man, and I can smell damned atheism when I find it.'

The scrivener opened his mouth to say something but Bull cuffed him on the temple, hard it seemed, for the man fell forward nursing his head. He was lifted, still dazed, to his feet. 'You are coming with us to Bridewell,' said Bull, smiling.

'God,' said the scrivener.

I carried his jerkin and mantle for him.

We travelled through Ludgate to prison, the scrivener walking between Bull and Talbot while I, at the rear, cast my eye over the document that Talbot had produced in Cheapside. I recognised its Arian heresies from my sizar days at Cambridge. It was an imprudent libertine who had copied them out for his perusal, but it was not the scrivener, for I had marked his deliberate hand and this lettering did not resemble it.

In the courtyard at Bridewell, while Bull led his charge to a cell (and thence, for the Privy Council was impatient, to the question), I stopped to kick dung from one of my boots and saw Talbot in conversation with a man I did not recognise. The fellow, very dark and ill-favoured, with cheeks molten-set by a childhood pox, did all the talking and Talbot listened intently, his head bowed, with something in his aspect most unfamiliar to me that spoke of deference and eagerness to please.

Two hours later, the prisoner was hoisted to the dank ceiling by his arms. Goaded by the agony of his dead weight, he acknowledged the heretical document as having belonged among his papers. I was on hand, with pen and dwindled inkpot, to set the confession down. It was dark in the cell and my hand was not as steady as I would have wished. I carried a candle to the board and wrote on the document: '*Vile heretical conceits denying the deity of Jesus Christ our Saviour, found amongst the papers of Thos Kyd, prisoner.*' Thereupon, I looked up and found Harry Talbot seated and Bull at bay. The scrivener moaned on the floor. He would have curled, I swear, into a ball like a hedgehog, had it been possible.

'It *is* yours,' Talbot was saying. 'You have confessed it. Do you wish to retract your confession?'

Bull took his cue and began to open the render: this very showily and with great clanking of metal.

'It was amongst my papers,' the scrivener cried, 'but I wrote it not.'

'Who did?' Talbot leaned forward. 'Was it the same man who wrote the libel in the Dutch churchyard? The playmaker Marley?'

The scrivener lifted his eyes in surprise at the name. He hesitated, then shook his head. Bull tugged at his ragged shirt and the prisoner barked '*No, no,*' like a pug.

'You shared a chamber together,' said Talbot.

'Two years ago!'

'You wrote for the same company of players. Come, we know everything. You are a familiar of this Marley.'

Bull dragged the man as he would a sack of oats. I took my pen to one of the lamps in the wall. The nib, as I suspected, was somewhat broken and I set to sharpening it with my poniard.

'Help yourself,' said Talbot. 'Help *us* to help you. If yours is not the hand that wrote these lines, whose did? Who is the damnable atheist for whom you suffer — who even now sleeps blithely in his bed?'

There: I split the fresh point and it was good again. I made sure of it against the light and waited to be of service. The scrivener was wailing, yowling rather, like a tomcat, and though his captive claw could not stir in the render, yet his scrawny body twisted and squirmed, his feet danced on thin air, he looked, with swollen jelly eyes, at the damage being done, he looked away, he near swooned. Many times had I witnessed a prisoner's incredulity, his *refusal* to believe what was happening to him. The love of God was more real than these agonies, yet the wretch persisted in his denials.

'Bull,' I said, 'enough for now.'

The scrivener sobbèd to feel the render yield. There was a stink from his breeches. 'Oh mercy, mercy I beg you…'

'That is the tool,' Talbot said, instructing Bull not yet to release the hand, 'of your ignoble trade. Doubtless you wish to keep it.'

The scrivener said nothing but stared, his eyes wide like a hare's, at his bloodied extremity. Bull bestirred himself, extracting from his apron a carving blade, very bright and doted upon. 'I could be let loose on these,' he said, 'and I should fashion me a fine pair of Kyd gloves.'

'Not my hand, good my lord!'

The scrivener was released from the render. He fell moaning to his knees, cradling his damaged hand. Talbot then, with that softening touch I so feared, gave him water to drink and addressed him kindly. 'This can all cease,' he said. 'Testify that this document belongs to Kit Marley. We already know it is so. We are all friends speaking freely.'

At this instant I witnessed the action of God's grace. In the midst of pain's tempest, the Devil's grip on his prey weakens; obdurate error lifts, like a cloud, and true repentance as the sun follows. 'It is Marlowe's,' said the scrivener.

'What's that you say?'

'Marlowe. He must… have written it out. It got shuffled among my papers.'

'He is a misleader of men, is he not? He preaches unbelief and his wit is turned against God. Tell us more, Thomas.'

Talbot's use of his Christian name provoked the prisoner to weep. Now the truth poured from him: a great flow of purging words, the putrid matter from his corrupted soul.

'Ward,' said Talbot, 'are you setting this down?'

I assured him that I was, though given the darkness of the cell the testimony would have to be written up again later.

'It was his custom,' said Kyd, 'in table talk or otherwise, to jest at the divine scriptures.'

'Go on,' said Talbot.

'Oh... He jibed at prayers. In argument he strove... to frustrate and confute what has been spoke or writ... by prophets and such holy men.'

'Give instances,' said Talbot, while my newly sharpened pen cut into the paper.

'When I said that I would write a poem about the conversion of St Paul... Marlowe said that he was a juggler and that I might as well write a book of fast and loose.'

'Did he traduce Our Saviour?'

'He would report St John to be Our Saviour's Alexis.' This I struggled, as I do now, to set down, it did offend me so. 'He said that Christ did love him with an extraordinary love.'

There was more, though I do not care to recall it. At length the prisoner grew faint and was led from the chamber to prison. Bull yawned and remembered his own pain. Harry Talbot was jubilant as he bade us good night. I followed Bull, restored to his groaning, out of the Bridewell into a cooling breeze. I had with me the atheistical tract. On the morrow I would add – for the sake of thoroughness – '*which he affirms that he had from Marlowe.*'

I, that have witnessed confessions and set down the truth that is meant to come from suffering, must own to a secret. I did go to the theatre once. It was The Rose, Kyd's theatre, of fanciful name given the stink from soap-boiling and the tanners' yards. I had not frequented – let me insist – the alehouse or Paris Garden beforehand: I am able well enough to resist *those* vices. But the crowd that flowed into the wooden O, the faces bright with anticipation and the sweet smell of currants for sale, turned my head, overcame my irresolution (for I knew that I should leave the Liberties at once, before temptation of the unreal snared my senses) and I paid for a space on a bench. People, high and low, breathed the same air, and men pressed against women unknown to them in the aptly named pit. Yet when the trumpet sounded and from the doors at the back of the stage erupted the players – Strange's men – all distraction ceased. A man claiming to be Machiavel came to the edge of the stage; he fixed the groundlings, that fixed him back, and spoke, and all the world beyond the theatre vanished. It was the tale of Barabas, the murdering Jew. For a little span of time, Time stood still: we had the commanding of it, for the players with only their bodies and the rolling lines of the play did weave a seeming world from nothing. Men and women in the audience jeered, they quarrelled with Barabas and cheered when he came to a fitting end. I could see through the imposture: the playmaker bought license with his moralising, though the theatre is a foundry of vice and illusion. Yet I was spellbound and became aware of the great ache in my back only when the dance was done, the actors withdrew, and with all the people I returned to myself and the world.

Five days after Kyd had made his confession, a warrant was issued for Christopher Marlowe's arrest. And so I came to glimpse the author of the play I had seen. He was brought back from Scadbury by Henry Maunder, not in chains but walking free: a gentleman, with light russet beard and dark, womanly eyes. He did not see me where I sat, mixing ink at an open window. He said something I did not hear (though he must have been apprehensive) and Henry Maunder laughed unguardedly. I tried to loathe the poet for his heresies. He was one of Sir Walter Raleigh's creatures, in whose rooms at Durham House he was said to preach against religion.

When Marlowe had passed in the courtyard, on his way to a coach and thence the Privy Council, I sought out my superior where he rested. 'That is but air and tongue waving,' said Talbot. 'Rumour is not enough to expose the power behind that school of atheism. We must shore it up with this playmaker.'

'He was not in irons,' I said, feeling oddly exultant.

'He has a champion in the Privy Council. They will go at him gently – for a time. But he may yet be brought to the question.'

Days passed, occupied with minor cases: disloyal boasts, or men who had blurted heresies in their cups and were reported for them. Most confessed at the very sight of Bull's implements. Harry Talbot was foul-tempered all the while. He said Kit Marlowe was reporting to the Privy Council daily, but nothing appeared to work. He wriggled free of allegations concerning the libels in the Dutch churchyard, that his plays had been used as incitements to unrest, even that he wrote the words found in Thomas Kyd's lodgings – offering a sample of his handwriting to prove the discrepancy.

'You do not believe this Marlowe wrote the Dutch libels?'

'He inspired the rogue that did. People love to see bloodshed on the gallows or the stage.'

'But it is not shed,' I replied, 'on the stage. Only in shadow.'

'A poet's words deceive,' said Talbot, 'so we are *undeceivers*. Sooth, some of my charges, when put to the question, have come to love me as their ghostly uncle. The Privy Council will get no truth from Marlowe for they are soft with him. Heresy is easy to maintain when the belly is full and the body at ease. But it soon peels away when correct pressure is applied.'

'He must look to his Maker,' said Bull merrily.

Talbot smiled to hear his dictum repeated. 'Earthly flames are better,' he said, 'if they lead to repentance, than eternal fire.'

This has to be believed. What mercy obtains in letting a man destroy his soul? Walking home that evening, I recalled the words of my superior when, following my first taste of his methods, whereat I quailed and clumsily wrote, he led me from the Bridewell to a lodging-house and sat me down with a warm posset. 'These pangs you feel are good,' Talbot had said. 'I do not trust the physician who feels no kinship with his patient. And as *his* task is the feeling of pulses, so *ours* is the feeling of minds. If in a man's complexion we find malady, we draw up the receipt – we bleed and purge. Oftentimes we may spare the knife, for the mere prospect of treatment will cure a lesser sickness. So be of good cheer, John, and resolute. We are not butchers but surgeons.'

No progress was made in the investigation. From pursuit of a libel, matters changed course and now heresy was the quarry. I attended to my scrivener's task of recording the prison's dealings. It was not my intention to hear Talbot talking with a guest in his chamber, but they spoke loudly, and my ears twitched at the mention of a certain name.

'My Lord Essex on the Council,' said the visitor, 'is most aggrieved. He will have Marlowe a damned heretical atheist and hurt Sir Walter thereby. Tarnish his metal. Spoil his credit with Her Majesty.'

'They can fix no charge upon him?'

'None. He speaks wittily of leaving the service. Of devoting himself to poetry. We cannot have that. Marlowe escape and Raleigh go uninjured? Well, since he is too agile a coney for the Privy Council, he must be caught some other way.'

'Methought you said he was Cecil's man.'

'He has done dark work for him. But that is in the past. If Marlowe is called to account in these matters by legal prosecution, he may offer secrets of Sir Robert's. Loyalty has it limits, Harry. Both my Lord Essex and Cecil will profit if the poet's mouth is stopped.'

There followed a thud of empty tankards on a board, the hoarse scraping of chairs, and I realised with seconds to spare that the conference was over. I pushed with the flat of my hands off the wall where I stood, ear to the wood, and managed with a flustered and guilty look to be seated at my desk when the door opened and I recognised, stepping out, his hands fastening the buckle of his girdle, the man with whom Talbot had been speaking on the evening of Kyd's arrest. Dark-haired, with black eyes that moved slowly in an ooze of self-love, he acknowledged my presence with the faintest of nods. I knew nothing about him, though he was no gentleman to merit an effusive bow. I bade him good morrow.

'Ay,' he replied and, lifting the latch, stepped out into the prison courtyard. Harry Talbot emerged – proud-bellied and yawning – from his room. He stopped instantly at the sight of me and then continued out the door.

I followed. 'Who is that man,' I asked, as the visitor awaited the return of his horse.

Talbot did not meet my eye. 'His name is Skeres.'

'A colleague of yours?' Talbot gave no reply. Resolutely he watched the clouds above the Thames. 'Would he be one of the Queen's Messengers?'

Pricked by my questions, Talbot said: 'He is my Lord Essex's man.'

'And what does my Lord Essex require of us?'

'Of you, nothing.'

I persisted, though I knew it was foolish to do so. 'That playmaker will go free,' I said.

'Matters will take their course.'

'God's work still?'

Harry Talbot turned on me. 'There are currents at work here that need not concern you, flotsam. You serve your Queen and God. It is better to look away from intrigues. You will look away from this one.'

The dappled horse of Skeres was brought to him by one of the stable boys. He mounted it, did not look back to acknowledge Harry Talbot watching him, then rode to the gate. I caught sight of another man – powerfully built, a redhead – rummaging in his nostrils with an ungloved finger, seated astride a brown jade in the street outside the prison. He and Skeres nodded in mutual greeting as the gate was closed upon them.

'Who is that other?' I asked, stepping back inside lest Talbot should strike at my impertinence.

'That other,' he said, shutting the door, 'is called Ingram Frizer.'

★

These things took place years ago; shortly thereafter, I escaped from Bridewell to wear out my fingers at the Inns of Court. Why, then, do I feel compelled to set this down, when Skeres and Poley, the participants in what followed, are mouldering in their graves and only the wielder of the fatal blade is, to my knowledge, still living? Other actors are gone: Talbot to Bedlam, my Lord Essex to the traitor's scaffold. The playmaker Kyd did not long survive the ruination of his writing hand. Thus runs the world away. Yet I am possessed, for the first time in my life, to set down not another's words but my own, concerning a matter in which I was a very small player.

It was evening at the end of May when Harry Talbot burst rudely into my room. I was collecting oil for my lamp and my hand shook at his sudden noise, so that I spilled a little on my papers.

'A good thing is done,' he said. From his gait and loudness I could tell that he was drunk. 'Through the eye! He has gone, winking, to the Devil.' Quickly I moved the papers on my table to make room for his descending rump. 'John, my good man. We squeeze true words from dry sinners, is it not so?'

'What has happened?'

Talbot dragged his sword towards his lap and rubbed its pommel. 'Poets,' he said, 'sprawl on their cushions dripping honeyed lies on the world. Well, now there is one less.' I thought of the scrivener Kyd in custody. Had another prisoner strangled him to stop his groaning? 'He did wheak like a stuck pig.'

'*Who?*'

'The sodomite. From a prick in his eye. They will say it was done in self-defence – that hot-blooded Marlowe did pounce on Frizer in a dispute over the reckoning.' Talbot, swaying slightly, unsheathed an inch of his blade. It seemed hot in the prison, though the evening was cool and breezy. 'They met in Deptford. The house of Bull's cousin. I think he meant to fly the country. Live with the French, in their stink, scribbling his verses.'

'How died he?'

'Screaming.'

'His soul unshriven?' I felt the terror of it in my spine. Sent to blackest Hell without a chance to bethink him. 'Harry…' I was trembling with anger; it made me incautious. 'It is our task to cut spiritual corruption from men's souls. If we do not do this work from *mercy* —'

My better, or my worser, angel made me hold my tongue, and at length Harry Talbot's eyes lost their fearful aspect. He was sober enough, and played at softening, as I had seen him do a dozen times before a prisoner. 'You are tired,' he said. 'Go home to your good wife and daughter. Let them thank you for the roof you provide, and for their daily bread.'

I mumbled excuses and left. Outside, the main gate was open for a delivery of maslin bread. I sucked in my belly to pass the mud-stuck cart, keeping my head bowed before the tradesmen.

A damned atheist, a blasphemer and spy: one of dark politics' creatures darkly dealt with. It was no concern of mine. Yet I felt sullied to be in the world when that fount of words was extinguished. And in what manner! Drunk, with his anger upon him. Killed in the spirit as in the flesh.

'God,' I said, then knew not how to continue my prayer.

I walked away from Bridewell prison and all the souls there in torment or in dread of the same. I moved fast, until my lungs tugged at me and a sweat came on. My brow was damp and it felt first the breath of the river. Even as I rebelled in spirit, I knew that I would write out, thereafter, in elegant and official script, the pain-provoked confessions of Thomas Kyd.

I stopped on the bank to watch the ships at their trade and the little boats ferrying from shore to shore. I pulled tight my cape: was it the wind across the Thames that made me shiver? I looked down and saw, floating on the dirty water, its wings torn by unknown talons, the dishonoured corpse of a dove.

Confessions of a Tyrant's Double

1

THE PIGEON SHOULD HAVE warned me, but it was the widow who made me afraid. She was very fat, smelling of onions, with a hairy wart near her lip that I felt when she kissed my hand. Her son was a good boy, she said. He was her only help since her husband died. Spare his life, O Father!

I rescued my hand as gently as possible. 'God be with you,' I said. 'Do you think our Hero President strolls about town with a pigeon under his arm? Where are my bodyguards? Where is my armoured car?'

The widow stared. Was it not true that Our Beloved Leader sometimes walks among his people, like Haroun al Rashid, to understand their troubles? I bowed my head to expose my bald patch. 'I am not,' I said, 'who you think I am.'

At once the woman began to spit. She slapped my wrists and tried to kick me on the shins. She cursed me wildly, wishing horrible death on my family and my government. She would bring disaster on our heads.

'Be quiet,' I said in desperation. 'Or I will have your son executed.'

I left the scene very quickly, while a cab driver helped the fainting widow to the ground.

Back home, my beloved wife accused me of being a fool. Dark roses of anger bloomed on her cheeks. 'When he was the Deputy,' she said, 'you thought it was a good joke. Don't deny it! I saw you practice his wave in front of the mirror. Now, with everything that's happened, you're passing yourself off as the President!'

'I didn't mean to.'

'Did anyone hear the woman? Did anyone see you together? O Merciful God, you will be arrested for impersonation.'

'It wasn't intentional.'

'Then why did you accept that pigeon from the grocer? You have taken a bribe! On false pretences!'

In a television film this would have been the moment when policemen knock at the door. And so I remember it, though perhaps they came in the evening, as lamb and yogurt bubbled on the stove. They barged in, short stocky men in civilian clothes, and poked about our flat, dislodging photographs of our lamented daughter, demanding our papers and asking my wife, with momentary politeness, for two glasses of water.

'We understand you make crushed fruit drinks,' said one of the policemen, wiping his wet moustache.

'You torture fruit.'

'In a press.'

'In a mangle.'

'You crush them and drink their blood.'

'Please,' I said, as they rested their heels on my wife's cushions. 'Is it about the pigeon? We have not eaten it. It is in the refrigerator.'

'We are very grateful,' added my wife, 'to the President for our refrigerator.'

The policemen told us to shut up and sit down. One of my interrogators took out a little camera. I sat for my photograph and thought of those tribesmen who believe that cameras eat their souls. They took three photographs of my face straight on, then two left profiles and two right profiles. I stood up with my arms spread wide and nearly yelped when a fist jabbed my armpit and spat out a tape measure.

'Well done,' said one of the policemen to his colleague.

'What a find.'

When they had finished taking my measurements, the policemen warned me not to leave the village. They left — wiping their shoes on the doormat — and my wife leaned against me in the hallway. I could feel her breath on my throat.

My wife said quietly, 'You must shave off your moustache.'

I was reluctant to do it. A hairy fellow since I was twelve, I had sported it for thirty years.

'It is too provoking. Even I... sometimes... when we lie together, imagine that you are *him*.'

I obeyed my wife. The bathroom tap sputtered, then dribbled like an old man's nose. I winced as, with nail scissors, I cropped the tough hairs. I bled in tiny spots when I shaved the bristles and stared in dismay at my moustache's negative: a broad strip of pale, shocked skin.

It was, of course, a terrible idea. When the policemen returned, accompanied by a secret serviceman who chewed his nails and smelt of talcum powder, they panicked at the sight of me.

'You bloody fool! Stupid interfering goat lover!'

Roughly, with a flurry of desperate slaps to my head, I was bundled into a van outside. I could hear my wife pleading with the secret serviceman for my release. At least could she make me some food, or pack some clothes before I went?

The van sped along unglimpsed roads. Bent double in the rear, I was shaken like a pea in a laughing man's belly. You will think me a coward for relieving myself in my trousers when at last the van stopped in an underground car park. I was pulled through corridors that stank of bleach, down narrow stairs, and thrown into a kind of furnished cellar.

Too soon, my torturers came for me. I recognised the two policemen but they did not meet my eyes. Another man, in a white coat with a black leather case, I did not know. I was pinned back in my plastic chair while the medical man lunged at my face with his implement. It was a poisoned brush! He held it up to my nose!

I felt wet bristles on my upper lip and tried not to breathe.

I opened my eyes on a strip of gauze stretched between the stranger's fingertips. 'While *yours* grows back,' he said.

Newly moustached, and sweating on my plastic chair, I witnessed a merry parting in the cellar doorway. The policemen were smiling and thanking the makeup artist with hearty thumps on his back. Equally relieved, for he was to walk free, the makeup artist bowed and pressed his hand to his heart.

Restored to my face, I was taken to meet Our Beloved Leader.

2

After the palatial splendour (which could not, with all its rugs and fixtures, conceal a strange proliferation of cables), the room in which the President received me was very modest. It was not his office (few people have ever seen that) but a study lined with books on the subject of Joseph Stalin. The President stood up at his desk and stretched out his arm. I shook, and shook his hand. The resemblance, as you know, was remarkable. That reassured me about my chances, for whom, getting rid of his double, would not suffer a pang of his own mortality?

'Look at you,' he said. 'Are you sure my father did not spend time in your village before you were born?'

I laughed for my life. 'You look,' I said, 'even more powerful and munificent than you do on television.'

'That is true.' Our Beloved Leader lifted from his desk a Hermès tie and began to wind it about his neck. 'I am seeing journalists for lunch. From *Time* magazine. They will learn the truth about our country.'

'Our great country, Hero President.'

'I don't need to be corrected.'

When the President had plumped the knot in his tie, I was escorted from his study. Instead of being returned to my cellar, I was locked in an apartment of the palace complete with a bathroom and a most comfortable bed. I searched in vain for a telephone. There were no windows to help me guess my whereabouts.

Long after I had finished a cold salad lunch, I was taken back to the President's study.

That second meeting, being a little longer than the first, answered my unspoken questions. Our Beloved Leader was tired, he said, from driving the Americans about the capital.

He asked me, quite disarmingly, with his trick of simplicity, if I would be his stand-in. 'Of course I love my people greatly. But I am so busy building up the country that I cannot always be there for them.'

Against the shout of every nerve in my body, I said yes.

'I promise you many comforts,' said the President. 'All your needs will be attended to. I have professionals to train you in the finer details. You will have, on occasion, to meet guests before the cameras. Minor politicians, you know, European celebrities…'

Hastily I agreed and thanked fortune for giving me, almost, the face of her favourite son. But, Merciful and Compassionate Knight, what about my family?

'Your wife? Don't worry. She was telephoned two days ago and told to expect your return.'

Can you imagine my joy at this news? I could have kissed the hem of his jacket. In fact I was astonished how much he knew about me. With great warmth he asked after my mother: had she recovered from her painful fall? He knew all about my family origins, about my crushed fruits business, and I stammered as I answered his questions. Unsheathing his smile, Our Beloved Leader said, 'All that life is finished for you. Your wife, your mother, your crushed fruits, are dead so far as you are concerned.'

'Dead, Master?'

'The living are dead to the dead.'

'Please… Hero President… I don't understand.'

Our Beloved Leader fetched a plastic folder from the glass-covered table. He extracted several photographs of a car – of *my* car – mangled and burned out by the side of a road.

'You died in this accident, friend. Welcome to paradise.'

3

It was always obvious to me that Our Beloved Leader is a handsome man. His foes will not say so, for a man's enemy must be evil, and evil – as everyone knows – takes ugly physical form. But you should understand (you, who see in Our Beloved Leader only the features of a terrible father) that his great smile, as broad and white as an American film star's, has left many people weak at the knees. I too had been considered handsome in my time. But now my good looks did not belong to me. I had to learn to practice his smile and endure the attentions of his Lebanese dentist. I had to wear a wig to hide my baldness. And I would have to coarsen with age at the same time, and in the same ways, as my mighty template.

The inmate of a luxurious prison, I underwent basic training. The policemen who had discovered me were replaced by 'Kamel' and 'Karim', tribal kinsmen of Our Beloved Leader, who, as my keepers, were to oversee my shadow life. 'Kamel', a very genial fellow inflated with pride for his obese daughters and a devourer of pistachio nuts – whose cases he discarded like a greedy parrot – would talk at me endlessly about his domestic life without expecting any response, as for want of a human ear one might address a dog. He would sit with me in a darkened room as I watched looped footage of the President to learn his walk and demeanour. 'Karim', who was as sullen as 'Kamel' was jolly, taught me how to imitate the President's gestures. These, as you know, have a stiff and excessive formality, adopted by Our Beloved Leader after his victory in the First Patriotic War. I had only to imagine myself under water, or wading through oil, to imitate him. The voice, however, came with difficulty.

'We need a professional,' said Karim, sucking the life out of a cigarette. 'Only a trained actor can teach him.'

I recognised the former television star the moment he entered the room. He nodded and smiled and looked as pale as curd. He despaired of my natural voice (a reedy tenor which I no longer have) and pulled at the greasy plumes of his hair. 'Can't you *hear*?' he shrieked. 'Can't you hear the bloody difference?'

Only by speaking all day in the President's voice was I able to make it my own. My back and shoulders began to ache from my walking constantly in his body. And then there was all the reading to do! As you know, Our Beloved Leader has produced hundreds of literary works – autobiographies, novels of adventure, political tracts and many articles for newspapers. Winning patriotic wars was not enough for his inhuman energies. I, his feeble double, barely managed to digest his writings or the gruel of his four-hour broadcasts, which I was forced to regurgitate in monthly tests set by fanatical Karim.

'We think now you are ready,' said Kamel, spitting pistachio, 'to make your first appearance.'

A government minister told me how, for the President's security, the police used sticks and electric rods to keep his admirers from getting too close. 'My cousin,' said the minister, 'wants to be among his people, but they are unhappy about the electric rods. *You* will be able to move more easily and shake hands with people, and we won't have to electrocute them so much.'

Being about the same size as their owner, I had two hundred pairs of shoes, three hundred suits and five hundred belts to choose from. Or rather, they were chosen for me and laid out neatly on my bed. Like the original, this false President was to wear hats lined with Kevlar. Always the routine would be the same – the day's costume set out on my bed, the bulletproof hat laid on my pillow.

We travelled for hours, in a convoy of 20 armoured cars, to the holy city of B. I stepped from the President's car into a tunnel of military green, and entered a courtyard to greet the faithful.

4

The Second Patriotic War saw me busier than ever. Along with my colleagues, whom I never met, I helped give Our Beloved Leader a godlike ubiquity. There were speeches to be delivered to jubilant crowds, visits to our recaptured territories, tours of the frontline to shake hands with trembling heroes. While the original President, from his several bunkers, oversaw the nation's defences, his doubles gave soldiers watches with their — I mean the President's — face on the dial, awarded cars to senior officers, and certificates for priority housing to the families of martyrs.

'Victory' ended with rebellions in the north and south of the country. All doubles were ordered to drive, without the usual escort, in open top cars to reassure the people that their President was safe. I was extremely nervous as I drove about the capital. Surely someone, maddened by the deaths of his sons in battle, would try to put a bullet in me? My Kevlar-lined hat could hardly protect my presidential face. Also, it was difficult not to pass other versions of myself on the deserted roads, presumed colleagues (for the President could not expose himself to risk) who like me hurried about on false affairs of state. How I longed, at times, to meet these men, my brothers, who alone would understand the misfortune of our privilege.

With insurrection crushed, life in the palaces quietened down. Our Beloved Leader expanded in self-assurance, and Kamel, with the bulging eyes and facial sweat of a momentary intimacy, handed me a plastic bag plump with pistachio nuts. 'These will fatten you up,' he said. 'I should know.'

It was my duty to keep up with the President's weight, so

food was brought to me by my keepers: all manner of delights unavailable to the people. I ate with a guilty conscience – I strained in marble lavatories – and watched myself swelling as though pregnant with *him*. The Lebanese dentist noticed the rot caused by so much eating and I suffered torture in his leather chair.

'Do you see how power changes a man?' said the dentist, while I spat pink saliva into a tray. 'You are still the man he *was*. But he is no longer that man. There is an air about him. He stands with one foot in a different reality, a new dimension.'

Having long ago mastered his gravity, I had now to emulate the President's levity. The looser, almost girlish wave, the maternal patting of his swollen belly, I copied directly from video footage. One morning, with Karim uncharacteristically delayed, Kamel switched on the television; he had become grotesquely fat – marooned in his body as I was in the President's – and prone to fits of giggling.

'Look at this!' he squealed. 'He has taken to dancing now!'

In the centre of a distended crowd – a throng of elderly men wearing tribal headdresses – a man who must have been the President thrust out his arms and pulled his knees, one by one, rhythmically towards his gut. He grinned broadly, his teeth clamping a Cuban cigar, as he performed a kind of victory dance. The absence of a soundtrack to accompany these movements made them seem all the more forbidding.

'Disappointments never get him down,' marvelled Kamel.

It was around this time, with half a million discharged and humiliated soldiers on the streets, that foreign workers began to die in large numbers. I was not unconscious, in the palace compound, of the sufferings of ordinary people, but what could I, the President's reflection, do in the world of substance?

Our Beloved Leader, addressing the same troubles, increased his guard to fifteen thousand.

5

You will surely remember what names the President gave himself around this time. He was our Knight. He was the Son of the People. Impressively, he was also the Father of the People. As for me, he was my twin brother and my creator. It is a paradox, I know. Accept it as proof of his power. He can order miracles. Monuments to the President's genius, to his wisdom, sprouted like the onions that people could no longer buy. I myself enjoyed the comforts of his vast new palaces, and continued to spread conscientiously, keeping up with his girth while the people sweated and starved.

Of life in our country, I have no need to tell you. But what about me, who never went hungry, who could expect medical treatment and painkillers, who lived in air-conditioned rooms? How did we, I mean I, cope with deception, in the perpetual night of these lies? I was unspeakably lonely. I had only my keepers, who expressed their hatred of Our Beloved Leader by hating his double. Violence was not their method for controlling me. My keepers made my life hard by making it soft – so close to what you, presumed reader, might dream of as the perfect life.

Women were brought to me. They did not know I was a double. By accepting their bodies I became indebted to my keepers. Following one dismal encounter (with the poor girl terrified at her knowledge of the President's impotence), I began to ask for women of a certain age; I specified their dimensions and, when they were delivered, called them by the wrong name, always the same name.

I tried, you see, to be a faithful husband. But I had never, in all the years we lived together, thought to discover the brand of my wife's perfume. And no woman brought to me in the humming darkness ever wore the right one. They had been doused in cheaper, more cloying scents, bubblegum for the nose. I could almost believe they were other – those naked doubles – than they really were, only briefly, so long as I did not breathe too deeply of their skins.

CONFESSIONS OF A TYRANT'S DOUBLE

★

My mother died one year after the war's end. I was forbidden to attend her funeral and for a week I had no public duties, my keepers judging it unwise to expose their grieving double.

Some things, however, could not be kept a secret. When the President's youngest brother, Mansur, shot dead a neighbouring president's bodyguard, no amount of activity from the secret police could keep a lid on the matter. So for a while Mansur was punished and sent to prison. There followed talk of a general amnesty for the country's prisoners. Our magnanimous President granted it and his crazed brother, along with thousands of others, walked free.

The encounter I had always most feared was ordered. I was to meet Mansur as he made his public act of contrition.

I was trained for the ceremony with a Mansur stand-in. I learned, as a robot is programmed, the gestures of brotherly forgiveness. And soon the stage lights were burning, the crowd's silence roared like a thousand lions. I watched the President's brother approach, smartly suited, his beard closely cropped and his prisoner's hair also. Television cameras purred to capture the scene. Feeble as a mouse beneath my mask of power, I received Mansur's humble and devout apologies. I accepted his cheque for blood money to satisfy the bodyguard's family. I grasped Mansur's paper dry hands to keep my own from trembling and kissed his alien beard.

When the ceremony was finished and I was drinking tea in a dressing room, I received a most unwelcome visitor.

'I've just discovered that you are a fake!' At the edge of his body, Mansur seemed to quake with rage.

'Please – young Master – I only follow orders.'

'I suffered *all that* for nothing?'

I contemplated falling to my knees and pleading for mercy. But Mansur seemed to lurch, to crumble like a wall of flesh, toward me. He pinched my arm. 'I like you so much better now,' he laughed. 'I was a contemporary of the President's brother. At university it was a joke how much we looked alike, and I got preferential treatment from our teachers. How long have *you* been duping people?'

Reluctantly I told him. He nodded, the false Mansur, and at once his mirth curdled. 'Did you ever guess,' he said, 'that we would be killed off in this manner?'

'Killed off?'

The young impersonator was being summoned by his keepers. Handing me his empty glass, he nodded. 'You know, *brother.*'

'Know what?'

'*We* do not exist.'

In the convoy back to the palace, I was staring at empty stalls and rubble in the streets when Karim, with a breath made sour by cigarettes and the cancer of which he knew nothing, whispered in my ear. 'You're not going to wobble now, are you, *Mr. President*?' I assured him, taking care not to turn my face from the window, that I was solid as a mountain. 'Wipe your eyes,' said Kamel, reaching past his colleague to press a handkerchief into my fist.

That night my keepers must have discussed tactics. In the morning they disturbed me at my hearty breakfast of stewed figs and chocolate. I had slept, not well but deeply, under a dreamless blanket of tranquilisers, and Karim had to repeat his news several times before I interrupted him with a bowl of spilling figs.

'It's not true! You are liars! I don't believe you!'

'Nevertheless,' said Karim smiling, 'these are the photographs of the happy occasion.'

I could not look. I would be sick all over the wedding guests. I glimpsed her face, small and dark, smiling not at me beneath her veil. The man beside her was disgustingly old. 'He is a good fellow,' said Kamel. 'He is a loyalist and of the right family.'

'A chief of police is better than a fruit crusher.'

I swore passionately at my keepers and could see Karim

coiling up to cough. I wished his disease on him. Impotent and jealous, I wept into my chocolate-soiled fingers.

I knew how the dead feel.

6

I was watching the evening news when my first blackout happened. I jumped up from my leopard skin chair, boiling and clutching my throat. I was choking on my swallowed self. The husband deprived of his beloved wife, the innocent seller of fruit juice, was trying to escape his living tomb. I sank into darkness – and hated the world for my recovery moments later, on the floor of my double suite.

I had to keep my infirmity a secret, though every room they put me in was surely bugged, if not filmed, according to custom. I did not know which to fear more: the rebellion of my forbidden self or my keepers' discovery of that rebellion. For the blackouts came at irregular intervals. They were not always violent. I would be eating lunch in my room with the hot sun on my eyes, only to look down at a plate of congealed sauce in a blue pool of evening light. I would top up with hot water my cooling bath and reach for the tap as the bathroom flooded. There was no telling when a fit would occur. I tried to concentrate on every waking second – as though my buried self crawled out whenever I relaxed my guard – and narrated my thoughts and movements to myself to ensure they would not give me the slip.

My stability was further undermined by the changing of my keepers.

Karim, who had been growing, if that's the word, alarmingly thin, collapsed one day in a palace forecourt and died in hospital three weeks later. His body betrayed him as I have betrayed my body. And then Kamel, whose fits of hilarity made him unstable, was pensioned off to the countryside to grow pistachios, leaving me in the clutches of his replacements.

These new men terrify me. I know nothing about them, not even their aliases. They are inhuman: non-persons, automatons of malice.

The new keepers sensed my reluctance to appear in public. Trained to cause injuries that leave no mark, they put me through a quick apprenticeship in pain. I was still wincing at the barbs in my stomach when I took up this pen. Like the woman crying her sorrow into a hole in the ground, I bleed onto this paper.

We live in a country where those things most dreaded almost always happen:

I blanked out.

In a mosque.

Disguised as the President, I contemplated my palms in prayer and woke up surrounded by a wall of soldiers. Our Beloved Leader sickens! I could hear the dread of the faithful as they shuffled from the mosque into the arms of persuaders outside. Happily my prayers were not televised. No appearance, by a double or the original, is *ever* transmitted live. So only those in attendance needed to be silenced. Am *I* to blame for their bruised ribs, for their frazzled scrotums and sweating hush beside their fretful wives? They saw a man who does not exist slump over a prayer mat. They must suffer for witnessing a shadow's fall.

Other blackouts have followed. Each one eats up the time I have left. And then it remains a matter of days before you — suspected snooper — discover these pages and my license will be all used up. Until then, I have a routine of insecurity to live by. Nobody knows in which palace the President sleeps, so the same movements are required for his look-alikes. On rare occasions I dream of myself, not myself, doubled many times, as in a fairground hall of mirrors, criss-crossing a ruined city, occasionally glimpsing myself, ourselves, in the backs of speeding cars, on our way to wakefulness in one another's bedrooms, to lie with shared sand between our toes. And certain thoughts, like flies, cannot be shaken from my head. Who can see through these doublings? A street magician jumbles up his pregnant cup with the cups that are empty. Who can tell which contains the marble? So among the soldiers who daily call me President, who can tell me apart from the original? What if *nobody* knows the difference? Could the President's powers be mine, if only I could escape my keepers? This is almost the face I was born with. Then why should I always be *his* double? Who can tell me he is not *mine*?

7

There is no going back now. I have thought the most forbidden of thoughts – a reflection's desire to be its object – and I have recorded them in this diary. The single hair (a trick I learned from a James Bond film) was detached from the binder where I had attached it, confirming your existence. So you have read the last instalment, palace spy, O loyal reader.

No doubt you are experiencing the latest catastrophe to strike our country. To confront the crisis I have, as you know, had a few public appearances to make. I have felt the damp palms of peace missionaries. If my daughter had lived, she might have envied me for meeting so many pop stars and actors and boxing champions. None of these photo opportunities will hold off the invasion. The Great Cowboy has declared his intentions and his armies are poised at our borders. What way out, in the teeth of the Great Power's resolution, for Our Beloved Leader?

Honestly – be honest – did you miss me those weeks when I was too busy to write? I rejoice, O subtle betrayer, at the possibility. For by your aid I have proved that I existed.

Everything henceforth may work itself out. My wife, without understanding it, will receive a big pension. Our Beloved Leader is always generous to the widows of national martyrs.

If my writing is hard to read, understand that I must hurry. My keepers are coming. Of all the President's doubles, the honour has been bestowed on me. Our world is about to change – though Our Beloved Leader, fled incognito to North Korea, will still enjoy his cigars after his corpse has been laid to rest.

I have been given the clothes for my balcony appearance. They are lying in front of me, laid out as usual on the bed. A beautiful Armani suit, a white silk shirt, a Hermès tie. Only the hat is missing. But let us not worry ourselves about fashion. The crowd is calling; the television cameras are ready for live transmission. I must comb our moustache. It is a great and momentous day in the history of our nation. Today, on the 28th of April, I shall appear before the great crowd celebrating my supposed birthday — and the sniper's bullet will find me, for it will come from a friendly gun.

Writers' Retreat

EDINBURGH — THAT GREY MAGISTRATE of a city, sombre and austere — wore a mask of carnival. Pavel had never seen it otherwise, although he felt he knew the city from the writings of Robert Louis Stevenson and Muriel Spark. From the top deck of the airport bus, he saw bungalows and offices, a zoo, then dark tenements and churches, until he reached the famous shopping street. He stepped off the bus into a festival crowd and, because she was pretty and smiled at him as if they were old friends, accepted the card handed to him by a young woman.

'We got four stars in *The Scotsman*. If you come tonight, there'll be jammy dodgers.'

Pavel made to hand the card back. 'I must go to Charlotte Square Gardens.'

'Keep it,' the young woman said, and turned her smile on others.

Pavel looked at the castle on its crags, trying to orientate himself from the map he had studied. Through vying currents of shoppers, festival-goers and performers, he wheeled his suitcase up Prince's Street until he found his turning. He saw the encampment of white tents behind iron railings. He walked towards his rendezvous.

Two days previously, he had sat at home with Anna in the purling cool of their electric fan, listening to the news on the BBC World Service. If we only switched off the radio, he thought, we would hear the dinking of the tram, the chatter of sparrows: the life of the city that knows nothing of politics.

'That settles it,' Anna said. 'You can't go.'

'I have an obligation.'

'To your ego.'

Pavel removed his spectacles and sighed. Neither wanted a row – it was not their way – yet the tension had built between them like the charge in thunderclouds.

'Getting out of the country's one thing. How do you know they will let you back in again? If they close the border –'

'It won't come to that.'

'We could stay with my mother. It might be nice: swimming in the lake, eating plums. You could work on that long poem.'

'With your mother at the other end of the table?'

'At least we'd be safe.'

'I've signed the contract. It's only a fortnight.'

'We could all be dead in a fortnight. Blown to bits like Luka in Sarajevo.'

'Luka was fighting on the frontline.'

'And where's our frontline going to be when the Russians invade?'

Pavel rested the bridge of his nose against his folded spectacles. 'I cannot let the English down,' he said, 'because of sabre rattling in Moscow. Go to your mother's, or stay with Elene and Merab. I promise I will be back. Even if I have to take a plane to Baku and hike the rest of the way.'

'I'd like to see that. You get a blister walking to the shops.'

Pavel considered his wife's expression. Her mockery often presaged a softening. 'I'll bring back some shortbread.'

'You'd eat it on the plane.'

'I would not.'

Anna's expression held. 'You are an obstinate man, and I am a very foolish wife. Don't expect to find me here if everything blows up.'

'It won't.'

'Obstinate!'

The silence lasted until nightfall. Only when the heat had begun to abate and the muezzin had recited the last *azan* of the day did Anna slope into the kitchen and fold her arms about his chest. 'Go,' she whispered. 'But don't promise to telephone every day, because you will forget, and I will worry.'

'Thank you, Annichka. I promise not to promise.'

He stood at the information desk, contemplating people as they ambled in and out. He could see boardwalks, a patch of grass with benches and chairs and readers in bovine postures of rest. The abundance of children surprised him; also, the flimsiness of people's clothing given the weather. He thumbed a text on his phone – *Made it! Kiss you, Pasha* – and was watching the spinning icon when a hand pressed his shoulder.

'Pavel! What a pleasure to meet you at last.' Sally Henderson's handshake was virile, a tendon crusher. His own, tempered out of consideration for her sex, seemed to him limp in return. 'I'm so glad you've made it. Still, you don't live in that part of the country, do you?'

'There is not time,' he said, 'to go to my hotel. My bags…'

'We can leave them in the Authors' Yurt.' He liked her compact figure, the pre-Raphaelite tangle of her red hair. She guided him to his complimentary tote bag and a lanyard, then led him into weak sunlight. 'Mind the loch,' she said of a puddle beside the boardwalk. Someone had launched a rubber duck upon it.

'That's the Spiegeltent. And the bookshop. I've already ruined myself in there. This is us.'

'I feel like Čingiz-khan,' said Pavel.

Inside the yurt, there were cushioned benches, a table laden with drinks, another with miniature pastries. Presumed authors stood with their presumed agents. In a side-tent, a literary hobo was granting an interview to a journalist.

'We have a big audience?'

'I asked at the box office,' said Sally. 'It's respectable. There aren't many opportunities to meet a poet from Akhmetistan. It helps that you've been in the news.'

'The Caucasus belli. Nothing like a Russian invasion to put us on the map.'

'Does it ever feel, sort of, wrong to write in Russian?'

'Kafka wrote in German. If he had lived another twenty years, he would have ended up in a German death camp. A language is more than the murderers who speak it.'

'I should tell you, in our audience there'll be a Scottish journalist who would like to speak to you.'

'Not about poetry.'

'Politics might come into it. I appreciate that could be awkward.'

'If I chant government slogans, it will be okay.'

'All the same, it would be good to get *some* publicity ahead of our book tour.'

Sally got up to fetch a sparkling water for herself and a whisky for Pavel, so that he was alone when Morag Finnie landed, like a nest-thrown fledgling, on his bench. 'I'm your chair,' she said. Blinking, he held her fleshless fingers in his hand. 'We're so lucky to be in the Writers' Retreat – it's a very intimate venue.' Gaunt, with a nimbus of white hair, Morag Finnie had to wet her lips before speaking. Pavel noticed her dancing eyes and the hollow skin above her clavicle.

'Interesting name,' he said. 'The place writers retreat to. The refuge, would that be correct? It is where you run away from your enemies.'

'Oh, you've no enemies here. Can I say how sorry I am about what's happening in your country?'

Pavel nodded.

'Your family is there?'

'My parents live in Moscow. I have a sister in Pittsburgh.'

'Petersburg?'

'No, Pittsburgh. Pennsylvania.'

'Well, that must be reassuring.'

Sally returned with the drinks and formally introduced them.

'By the way,' said Morag. 'I was stopped by a gentleman at one of the tables outside the Spiegeltent. An Akhmeti. He said he knew you.'

'Me?' said Pavel.

'Maybe he's one of your admirers.'

'I doubt that.' He swallowed the single malt and rapped at the fire in his chest. 'Please, excuse me.'

As he left the carpeted fug of the yurt, he heard Sally call after, 'Get him to buy one of your books!'

Pavel crossed the square, oblivious to the statue on its plinth and children running with ice creams. A man in an ivory suit and redundant shades waved at him from a deckchair.

'Pavel Maximovich, welcome to Scotland. Please, take a seat. There is time before your reading.'

'I sit too much. It goes with the profession.'

'I thought librarians were always on their feet.' The man stood up. His mouth looked wet in its black nest of beard. 'My name is Azer Masayev. I work at the consulate here in Edinburgh.'

'How very pleasant for you.'

'Yes, isn't it? In August, there is music, dance, theatre. There are poetry readings. Like yours, for instance. The beginning of a tour, I understand. It would have been remiss of me not to greet one of our most distinguished poets. Even if he does write in Russian.'

'Obliging of you,' said Pavel.

'It is my patriotic duty. We must support one another in these difficult times. Did you know that civilians are fleeing from the border? There are rumours that Russia will send in their Chechen battalions.'

'Please God that doesn't happen.'

'Please God.' Azer Masayev pinched the frame of his shades and removed them slowly. It looked to Pavel like a gesture practiced in a mirror. 'Of course, if we could, I am sure, we would both be fighting to protect our homeland. What's more natural than the instinct to close ranks against a common enemy?' The man's eyes were beautiful, thickly lashed. 'You're very quiet. I hope you get a second wind before your reading.'

'I am a patriot, Mr Masayev.'

'I have read your book. I must say, it's a most interesting selection of your work. One piece I did not expect to find.'

'You think sonnets are too finicky to translate?'

Azer Masayev opened his mouth in a mime of amusement. 'I am referring to a different poem. A satirical assault on the nationalist movement that liberated Akhmetistan from the Russian stranglehold.'

'You mean,' Pavel said, 'the defence of my language.'

'The language of our oppressor.'

'Which we are currently speaking.'

'The Kremlin's ambitions have fixed on language as the marker of ethnic identity. That gives them all manner of pretexts for intervention. We must not play their game.'

'I should have to stop publishing, then.'

'All we ask is that you take a clear line. Moderate your fetish for nuance.' Pavel spluttered. 'Wait, hear me out. You will insist that poetry has no borders, that politics demeans it. This is the indulgence of peacetime. In war, a nation must have one voice.'

Pavel looked into those tender brown eyes. 'Look,' he said. 'This is a fuss over nothing. Most people have more enthusiasm for picking their noses than they have for poetry. As a cultural form, it is of no consequence.'

Masayev raised an eyebrow. 'Why would you write, if that were so?'

'Maybe I have a compulsion.'

'A nation needs its anthems.'

'A nation needs the rule of law and a free judiciary. I'm sorry – my translator is waiting for me.'

'Don't let me detain you.' Masayev transferred his weight from one foot to another. 'Oh, before you go. Did you hear the sad news about Edvard Ananuri? It seems his house burned down. Everything in it lost — family photographs, his library. The manuscript of a novel he had been working on.'

A cavity opened in Pavel's chest. 'Is he all right?'

'Ananuri? The state will rehouse him. But we cannot rewrite his book.' Azer Masayev batted his handsome lashes. 'A friendly word of advice. Conflict changes things. They harden people. The same is true for nations: when life gets tough, they can no longer afford indulgences.'

'Edvard is harmless — a storyteller.'

'And his country will not abandon him in his need. Though Lord knows it will not be easy, given the number of refugees we are going to have to cope with. Pavel Maximovich, I am not asking much. In the course of your visit to Britain, you will have the ear of influential people. Writers, journalists. Given all that you owe your nation, we hope you will not make utterances that will bring it into disrepute.'

'Have you nothing more important to be doing?'

'As I say, a nation needs its poets.' Masayev folded his sunglasses and hooked them by one of the arms to his breast pocket. This, too, seemed a practiced gesture. *How difficult it is*, thought Pavel, *to live free of the examples set by cinema*.

'See you at the reading,' said Azer Masayev.

Under buffeted trees they stood, waiting to make their entrance. Pavel checked his mobile phone: nothing. He switched it off and attended to an eyelash that had bent itself into his right eyeball. The more he rubbed and blinked, the sharper became his discomfort, so that he was weeping lopsidedly when Morag Finnie gave the 'go' sign and the door opened to the smallest tent at the book festival.

Inside, a crimson carpet and a dais with microphones and a near silent audience of a dozen people. Morag sat on one end of the platform, Sally the other, and Pavel was the filling. A young man in an official tee-shirt fitted them with lapel microphones and Pavel stretched his neck like a gorilla submitting to grooming.

'It's not a bad turnout,' whispered Sally. 'There's your countryman, look. He must be a real fan.'

Pavel looked. In the front row, of course.

'Good afternoon, everyone. My name is Morag Finnie, I'm a historian at Edinburgh University, and it's my tremendous honour to be introducing the poet Pavel Kondrashov. Also with me is Sally Henderson, a poet in her own right, who has translated Pavel's poems into English. I understand that you worked on them together...'

'We corresponded by email,' said Sally. 'I'd send my rough translations, Pavel would comment, I'd make changes. Gradually we'd approach something we were happy with.'

'I am never happy with my poems.' Pavel heard the audience hum with amusement. 'Poets,' he said, 'are miserable people.'

'The book,' said Morag, 'is called *Home Fires*, it's published by Stone Book Press, and I have to say, it's a wonderful collection. There's a powerful sense of connection to the land. It's a book that breathes the fragrances of your native Caucasus.'

Pavel looked at Sally. 'Should I say yes?'

'Yes!'

'No.' This met with laughter. 'What I mean is, a book is just a vessel. It is marks on a page. *You* are the one who brings words to life. It is in *your* head.'

Morag Finnie's rictus had tension in it. She was, thought Pavel, too thin for levity. 'I should say,' she said, 'a few words about Pavel Kondrashov. He was born in 1969 in Kirill, the capital of Akhmetistan, to Russian immigrant parents. His father was a nuclear physicist, his mother a teacher. In 1989, he was imprisoned briefly, while studying at the University of Tbilisi, for writing an article in support of the anti-Communist uprisings in Eastern Europe. He got a degree in English Literature and returned to Akhmetistan, where he has worked as a farmhand, a forklift truck driver, and latterly as a librarian. His reputation as a poet is well established in his homeland and in Russia. Given the current geopolitical upheavals in

Akhmetistan, we are especially fortunate that he has been able to come here today. Will you please join me in welcoming Pavel Kondrashov?'

Pavel grinned into the applause. He looked over the gathered heads yet felt, like a magnet's pull, the lure of the ivory suit and the black beard. 'Perhaps,' he said, 'I will start with a few poems. I should explain...' Azer Masayev raised his left leg and poised its ankle on his right knee. 'I am Akhmeti but my parentage is from elsewhere. I write in Russian because it is my mother tongue. Because it opens to me a great literature. This is not without controversy, for obvious reasons.'

He dried. Sally leaned into his field of vision. 'I suppose,' she ventured, 'we have similar tensions in Scotland. Whether to write in Standard English or Scots, or even Gallic.'

'But you are not, uh, coerced. For many years, under Stalin, Akhmeti was not an accepted language. People were punished for speaking it.'

'Yes,' said Morag. 'Terrible. What would you say is the status of poetry in your country?'

'It is not important.'

'I always think,' said Sally, 'Russian speakers take their poetry very seriously.'

'That was before we had western television.'

'Is it,' asked Morag, 'one of the consequences of capitalism that poetry is no longer essential?'

'Ah – I have written about this.' He opened his copy of the book and quickly found a passage. 'Perhaps you could read it for me.'

Sally leaned in until their shoulders touched. 'This,' she said, 'is from Pavel's introduction.'

'The reader may be surprised to learn that I cannot entirely regret the marginalisation of poetry since the fall of Communism. Under the old regime, people valued good poetry if they could find it, because they were desperate to know that some sort of truth might survive the lies. People also read a lot of very bad verse, because that was what the system produced. Yes, it is true that Pushkin was loved in the USSR – because the USSR made him the object of a veneration cult – but his works were read through lying eyes. They were co-opted, misinterpreted, glossed over, and across the whole enterprise fell the gulag's shadow, so that Osip Mandelstam could observe, 'Poetry is respected only in this country. There is no place where more people are killed for it.'"

Pavel found him in his customary place beside the fountain, in the jigsaw puzzle shade of a plane tree. Edvard was feeding pigeons from a paper bag.

'Lord Byron is dead. The one with a clubfoot.'

Pavel sat down. 'Perhaps he is on holiday.'

'Pigeons are entrepreneurs – they don't take holidays.' The old man shook crumb dust from his bag.

'People say they bring diseases.'

'People bring diseases.'

'Do you give them all names?'

'What, do I look crazy to you? Only some.'

'Those with stubs for feet and one eye missing.'

'You have to admire them for surviving.' Edvard cooed at the pigeons. 'And how are you, my young friend?'

'Surviving.'

'Any new work?'

'Doggerel, mostly. I want to thank you for giving us dinner the other night.'

'My pleasure.'

'Anna and I would like to invite you back. It won't be much of a feast.'

'Have they still not paid your salary?'

'Not this month.'

Edvard stroked the deckle edge of his paper bag, then crumpled it in his fist and stowed the ball in his trouser pocket.

'We need a garden,' said Pavel. 'What do you think? Grow some vegetables. Keep a chicken.'

'One chicken? Don't get ambitious.'

'The eggs would be welcome. A bit of protein. Honestly, Edvard…'

'I know.'

'I had to sell my books.' It was hard to meet the look in the old man's eyes. 'Anna thinks she might have a job. Selling perfume to gangster's wives.'

'Door to door?'

'In an actual shop.'

'Ah,' said Edvard, 'the rewards of having a doctorate in philosophy.'

They sat for a while on the bench, watching traffic. 'How are things with you,' asked Pavel.

'I gave a reading in a school the other day. Sometimes I wonder if everything I published is contaminated with the times I lived in. My books smell of fear, they smell of compromise. Even if they are about happy children on a Black Sea holiday – or talking squirrels.'

'Talking proletarian squirrels.'

'The squirrel is a pioneer! The squirrel is a Stakhanovite!' Edvard's laugh had grit in it. 'If you want books, you can borrow mine.'

'Thanks.'

'In the old days I might have put a word in for you with the Writers Union.'

'Even if there were such a thing now, I write in Russian. They wouldn't give me a job cleaning toilets.'

'You could always write in Akhmeti.'

'You think I haven't tried?'

Squabbling broke out in the branches above them. They looked up.

'The crow, on the other hand, is a capitalist.'

'Those are magpies,' said Pavel.

'Magpies are crows. I want to tell you something.'

'Yes?'

'I am thinking of writing a letter – no, a series of letters – to the media. Concerning our president.'

'Your old school friend.'

'Someone I know knows someone – her neighbour – who did, shall we call it, freelance work on the president's behalf when he was still a Party man. This neighbour of my acquaintance, this unofficial employee, was a killer.'

'A what?'

'A killer.' Edvard's eyes softened at the sight of a sparrow taking a dust bath beside the overflowing municipal bin.

'Are you saying...?'

'I am not saying he killed anyone for the president. During the Wild West years, he was a sort of sheriff for him, knocking heads together.'

'Do you have any evidence?'

'I think so.'

'Edvard: is this wise?'

'No. I am old and I have only bad books for Communist children to show for my time. I think perhaps I could do something...'

'What makes you think the press will publish?'

'There are newspapers in other countries. Russia, for instance.'

It was a hot day already, but a second, inner sun scorched Pavel's chest. 'You can't be serious,' he said.

'Can I not?'

'The Kremlin hates our nationalists. Any revelations crossing the border via *Pravda* or *Izvestia* would be dismissed out of hand as Russian propaganda.'

'Obviously, I would prefer the facts to come out in this country.'

'I think you'd be taking an absurd risk.'

Edvard shrugged and placed a hand on Pavel's wrist. 'Forget it. I'm daydreaming.'

'Seriously –'

'It is just an old man's fantasy of settling scores. I'm sure I won't do anything.'

'Now I really *am* worried.'

Edvard pressed his hands on his knees and got to his feet. Pavel watched him, still seated, still afraid.

'Let us go and have that beer,' Edvard said. 'Before beer is banned. Come on. It is shaping up to be a very hot day.'

Pavel was warm now, in his only suit, under the scrutiny of eleven strangers and one new acquaintance. He saw, at the edge of his vision, Morag Finnie lift a slender hand to her throat. Sally sat with their book in her hand, the fan of its pages aflutter.

He thought of Edvard. He thought of Anna. In the front row, Azer Masayev uncrossed his legs.

'My first poem,' he said, 'I will read in translation. It has no title: just the first line.

As rivers thirst for the sea
I thirst for you, my homeland:
Not for the beat of martial drums
Nor the grievous flutter of flags
But for the roll of familiar names,
The spangled dance of a chestnut's shade
Across a square where my schoolmates played
In my homeland when I was young.

As rivers thirst for the sea
From far afield I long for home:
Not for the mawkish patriot's song
Nor the lash of the statesman's tongue
But for the lap of Black Sea waves,
The whispering of an old hornbeam
Above the peal of a glacial stream
In my homeland when I was young.

As rivers thirst for the sea
My verses tend towards their source:
A donkey brays, the muezzin chants,
The dusty summer runs its course,

Some oleanders bloom among
The fragrant jasmine that enchants
The honeybee into a trance,
In my homeland where I was young.

Even as the oleander
I am rooted in this soil:
Transplant me and I'd meander
Hopelessly in fruitless toil.
Yet don't confine me to one song,
Your angry dirge of 'Only This':
I am *And*, I am *Also*. Bliss
Cannot withstand a cult of wrongs.

My country is Akhmetistan
It is also the Realm of Books:
I am the almond blossom and
I am Onegin's tragic looks.
These sun-baked hills are home to me,
Though Russian drifts of snow may heap
Up from the company I keep
In the Free State of Poetry.

As rivers thirst for the sea
I thirst for you, my homeland:
The rhythms of your native speech
Complement my Russian tongue,
The hidden chord whence music comes
Unbidden as the rains in spring
That gave new life to everything.
In my homeland when I was young.

A pause, while the audience assured itself that the poem was
finished, then a bloodless and polite murmur.
'Thank you,' said Morag.
Azer Masayev's mouth disappeared into his beard. He

folded his arms and stared at his polished shoes.

'That is,' said Pavel, 'my attempt in English. This next poem I read in Russian.' He turned, with a nod at Sally, to the piece with which they had agreed to begin.

A table awaited them in the bookshop with copies of *Home Fires* arranged like a flimsy barricade between the author and his public. Pavel and Sally sat and waited.

'I think – yes,' said Sally, 'she's coming this way.'

A middle-aged woman, rosy-cheeked with broken capillaries, approached the table. She glanced at Pavel. 'Very nice,' she said.

'Yes?'

'Beautiful language.'

'Thank you.'

'I wonder if you wouldn't mind...' The woman addressed these words to Sally, presenting her with a slim paperback.

'Oh,' said Sally. 'That's one of *mine.*'

'Would you mind signing it for my daughter? She wants to be a poet.'

'My condolences,' said Pavel.

'If you could make it out to Angela with a G.'

Sally blushed as she uncapped her pen. 'Of course. I'd be delighted.'

Pavel had only one audience member to speak to.

'That was unhelpful, Pavel Maximovich. However, not too much harm was done. You were not addressing multitudes.'

'Poetry is intimate: it is not suited to the mob.'

'There is a journalist who wishes to speak to you.'

'How do you know?'

'She told me herself before your reading.' Azer Masayev glanced at Sally and continued in Akhmeti. 'You said a great deal with your silence. Not one mention of your country's looming invasion by a foreign power.

'I think that is common knowledge.'

'You would do well to be less evasive with the British press.'

Pavel allowed himself a sigh. 'It is to the credit of our homeland that the words of poets still merit attention. Here in Britain, no one shows the slightest interest.'

'Perhaps you would like to live here, then, where your ingratitude can have no consequences?'

Masayev's mild expression was a provocation. Flushing, and powerless to disguise it, Pavel whispered, 'You *know* where my home is.'

'Yes – and I know how it suffers while you enjoy the hospitality of the British Council.'

'What's happening is in my heart every time I open my mouth to read.'

'Lip service,' said Masayev.

'It's the *truth*.'

The consular official showed a sharp pair of incisors. 'You may think you're the only intellectual here, that you are wiser and more sophisticated than paper pushers like me, but you are not the only one to have read books. What is Satan's motto in your Bible? *Non serviam*: I will not serve.'

'So this is what it's all about. The Akhmeti Writers Manifesto.'

'A simple gesture of solidarity.'

'I cannot sign a letter that condemns –'

'Your people. The Russian people.'

'Did you not hear – I mean really *hear* – the poem that I read?'

'Rootless cosmopolitanism.'

'That was a phrase in Soviet times, comrade.'

'Gestures count in moments of crisis, and the gesture you made back there was unambiguous.'

'How I wish that were true. Then you would not be angry with me.'

'I am not angry, Pavel Maximovich. Only disappointed.'

Pavel watched Azer Masayev turn and walk elegantly, in his ivory suit, with his consular assurance, out of the tent.

'What was that about,' asked Sally.

'A literary disagreement.' Pavel took care of his breathing, as Anna had taught him, and waited, conscious of Sally's solicitude, until the blur of the world resolved into detail. 'Well,' he said, 'I think we have come to the end of our fan base.'

'Wait a bit. Others might turn up.'

Morag Finnie joined them, smelling of cigarettes. 'I thought the reading was a *great* success,' she said. 'I heard some really complimentary comments on the way out. Has there been a good take up here?'

'We are *fighting* them off,' said Pavel.

She looked towards the exit. 'Was that your countryman you were talking to just now?'

'Hardly.'

'But didn't he –'

'My country people are here. Do you say country people?'

'You can.'

'Readers. At the International Book Festival. And now,' said Pavel, 'let us go for a drink. Perhaps we can ask that journalist if she would care to join us…'

In My Father's Garden

HOME » GARDENING » GARDENS TO VISIT

Little Spinney

Ken Godfrey remembers the creator of an eccentric and enchanting garden.

It was with great sadness that I learned this week of the death of Gerald Surfleet, the celebrated Harley Street doctor and biographer of Andrew Marvell. With his ripe wit, sporting talent and extensive wine cellar, he was a good person to count as a friend. I will remember him best for his idiosyncratic contribution to English gardening.

Amidst the heaths, pines and executive houses of east Berkshire, Gerald Surfleet created Little Spinney: seven acres of pure fantasy, divided into nine garden rooms, each inspired by a stanza from Marvell's poem 'The Garden'. These included a rill garden, a knot garden and an orchard stocked with ancient English apple varieties.

I remember visiting the scrubby wilderness – a great tangle of brambles and gorse, loud with the shrieking of children – when Surfleet was pegging out his future legacy. The early years were a riot of colour: asters and aquilegias, foaming borders of phlox and, in late summer, fireworks of agapanthus. Surfleet imposed a superstructure of topiaries and yew, with areas of paving and formal water. Follies began to creep in: the odd Grecian urn, an obelisk, a copy of a Roman bath spilling over with poppies. Surfleet had an artificer's knack for creating illusions, leading the visitor along suggestive, winding paths. In the early nineties, he extended the garden when he bought a neighbour's smallholding. There, where prosaic marrows had fattened, he created his loveliest spaces: the canal and sundial gardens and an azalea punchbowl.

My friend paid a high price for his devotion to horticulture, his wife, the actress Heda Surfleet, leaving him in 1980 and taking his two children with her. Yet I never heard Gerald complain about his loss. Perhaps it suited him to wander solitary in his creation. As Marvell wrote, "Two paradises 'twere in one / To live in paradise alone."

He was not alone for long, however, as a growing number of enthusiasts began to visit the garden, enchanted by its chromatic palette. The highlight, in the nineties, was a dazzling array of asters, eclipsed in the new millennium by an enviable collection of Victorian roses. Yet the garden was more than the sum of its parts. It was constantly evolving, a horticultural daydream, with unfamiliar vistas and fresh curiosities revealing themselves at each visit.

It is hard to believe, given the vigour of the man, that Gerald Surfleet is no more. He left us too soon, but did so with the knowledge that his legacy is secure. A five-person trust, including his son who inherits the house, will oversee the preservation of Little Spinney for generations to come.

*

Hi Nick. Looked for you in the nursery. Hope this finds you. The plants I require: wall germander, thyme, green sage, marjoram, myrtle, *lavandula x intermedia*. Can you get your hands on plenty of broken terracotta?

Best to you & Helen.

Mark S.

IN MY FATHER'S GARDEN

★

To: Hugo Pickthorn, Andy Coates, Victoria Beazley
Subject: A knotty question!

Dear fellow trustees,

For reasons that will become obvious, I have not used our Google Group address for this email. It gives me no pleasure to be surreptitious, but given recent behaviour from Mark, I think it better to be discreet. I am sure it cannot have escaped your attention that the knot garden at Little Spinney has been tampered with. Actually, tampering is an understatement: I walked there yesterday and saw to my dismay that one of the knots has been dug up completely! The bare earth was quite a shock. I am certain that the box showed no sign of disease. Hugo, might you have a word? After my recent exchange with Mark, I feel a polite but firm letter from the chair would have more effect.

Wishing you all a very pleasant Bank Holiday weekend,

Marjorie

★

Dear Hugo. Thanks for your letter. Rest assured that the knot garden is safe. I'm making it more authentic. *Buxus sempervirens* was an innovation of the C18th & pebbles for the unplanted spaces = anachronistic. With new planting and terracotta, I am adding a sense of history & aroma. Best wishes, Mark

P.S. Hope you like the saucy postcard. From Dad's collection of Donald McGills.

★

To: Hugo Pickthorn, Andy Coates, Victoria Beazley
Subject: More innovations

Dear fellow trustees,

I went this morning to check on the 'progress' of the knot garden. I was reassured to a degree: the pattern has been restored, although I preferred the clipped box to Mark's amalgam of aromatics. I do wonder whether our acceptance of these changes is in keeping with our obligations to the Trust.

I should like to draw your attention to another development in Little Spinney. You may have noticed the proliferation of log piles. I know very well what purpose these serve, but while beetles may like them, garden enthusiasts are liable to find them unsightly and out of keeping with Little Spinney's character.

I spoke to Tom Atkins about his work under the new regime. He was loath to complain, but did mention the challenge of maintaining the garden without chemical fertiliser. There are certain areas for which Mark shows no enthusiasm: he is, for instance, 'not that fussed' (his words, apparently) about his father's roses. Consequently, the labour of manuring them falls exclusively to Tom. This, it seems to me, is no way to reward him for his decades of loyal service.

Yours in concern,

Marjorie

*

To: Nick Haggerty
Subject: Fancy some topsoil?

Hi Nick, please find my shopping list attached. I plan to restore heather to Little Spinney. As for the lawns, time to put them back in nature's hands. I'll be selling topsoil if you've a use for it. Maybe we could do a trade. I need plenty of wildflower seed.

Must dash: I have a man coming round who collects smut.

Regards to Helen.

Mark

★

To: Hugo Pickthorn, Andy Coates, Victoria Beazley
Subject: Upping our game

Dear fellow trustees,

I am writing this in the early hours of the morning, as I am quite incapable of sleep. Yesterday, I spent several hours in Little Spinney. I found brambles bursting out of the yew hedges and dragging at the azaleas. Many of the flowerbeds have been given over to nettles and dandelions. The urns are succumbing to goosegrass and the obelisk is disappearing under ivy. As for the orchard, it is in a lamentable condition, with carpets and rugs mouldering over the grass. Tom Atkins tells me that this eyesore is part of a plan to turn the orchard into a 'forest garden'. Tom further informs me that there are plans afoot to close off two paths and to block up the view from the rill garden to the farmhouse. It is in reaction to these developments that I have seen fit to write to Mark Surfleet. Please find a copy of my letter in the attachment.

Yours as ever,

Marjorie

★

To: M. Truscott@yahoo.co.uk
CC: little-spinney-trustees@googlegroups.com
Subject: Various

Dear Marjorie,

Thank you for your letter. I hope you won't mind my responding electronically: I am of that generation which finds it hard to think when writing by hand. Also, as you will appreciate, the disposal of my father's library (did he ever show you round, I wonder?) is taking up a great deal of my time, and I can type faster than I can scrawl.

I appreciate the sincerity with which you express your concerns about alterations at Little Spinney. However, I must say that I find some of your observations a little excessive. I have not allowed nettles and brambles to 'run rampant' through the azalea garden, but nettles are a major food plant for butterflies and so I tolerate them where I can. As for brambles, there were swathes of them on the land when I was a child, before my mother took us to Scotland. I am partial – aren't you? – to blackberry jam.

You complain about my 'new regime' of low maintenance, but I think my father was a little too free in his use of glyphosate and difenoconazole. I suppose it was understandable, given his profession, that he saw fit to drug the gardens. This summer I predict fewer algal blooms in the canals: a direct result of the decline in nitrates. I consider a resident frog or palmate newt to be a greater ornament to Little Spinney than swathes of chemically doped flowers.

Elsewhere in your letter, you complain that I have let the cypresses grow too high in the sundial garden. I agree, which is why I plan to remove them before they plunge the site into shadow. As for the obelisk, ivy is indeed climbing up it. I do not see this as anything more than the monument's 'bedding in' to its setting. As you, of all people, must know, Dad liked a picturesque ruin.

You raise two final questions, which I can answer quickly. Tom is getting close to retirement age. I do not want to encumber him with too many tasks, and we have to work within budget. And no, I will not be 'channelling the proceeds' from the sale of my father's library and cellar into the maintenance of the garden. The terms of the Will were perfectly clear: the garden is in trust, the house and contents are my and my sister's inheritance.

With best wishes,

Mark

P.S. I did not know that the pebbles had been your gift to Dad. I have them in a bucket: do come and collect them if you want.

★

To: Hugo Pickthorn, Andy Coates, Victoria Beazley
Subject: [No Subject]

Dear all,

I see from my inbox that you have received a copy of the outrageous email addressed to me by Mark Surfleet. He has spared me the task of forwarding you the same. I shall not comment on his dismissive and patronising attitude towards me personally. It is my hope that his letter will finally persuade you about the approach he plans to take to his father's legacy – and to those of us entrusted with maintaining it.

Marjorie

★

Little Spinney, 14th August

Dear Connie,

Happy anniversary to you and Ella! I've been imagining your celebratory picnic beside the lake. I hope the heat is less intense. Grim to think of Ottawa's forests going up in smoke.

Summer in England has been a more temperate affair: none of the droughts or floods of recent years. This is just as well, as Little Spinney in its present form is an unmanageable confection. It would be interesting – a Lord of Misrule summer – to let the vegetables come into flower and the wildlings sprout in the orchard. Why not let the self-willed seedlings put on their display, the poppies and foxgloves that Dad approved of so long as (like us) they knew their place? I find them more engaging than his collection of roses: fussy cultivars with scarcely a bee between them.

Speaking of Dad's collections, I've finally off-loaded his vintage erotica. Got a good price for it, which almost surprised me, given the infinite filth available to us on the Internet. I also had a valuer from Christie's take a look at the vases. They are seriously out of fashion, so maybe we should hold on to them until the winds of bad taste change.

Not much news otherwise. I rarely hear from Kathy, who's in New Zealand, probably in the arms of some Kiwi, and good luck to her. Been seeing a bit of Andy Coates. Had no idea he was so bitter about the loss of his land. We raided the cellar together and began to reminisce about the old days. I may have made some intemperate remarks, as by nightfall he was furiously convinced that Dad had played a part in the hiking of his ground rent. It is true that Dad was well connected: who knows what agreement might have been made on the golf course? Naturally, I tried to talk Andy down. He's a good bloke, but fouled up by life's disappointments.

This morning I saw a mole cross the cinder path. I stared after it – such an improbable sight, the half-blind lozenge of fur skittering out of its element until it found shelter under the yew – and I thought, Dad would have killed that little battler for the sake of his lawn.

Wishing you and Ella another year of happiness.

All my love,
M xx

P.S. Guess who's been dogging my every move. The other day, Marjorie Truscott battled through buddleia to warn me that, "at the current rate of decline, we will be dropped from the Yellow Book". I had to fight the urge to lift my hands to my face in pantomime horror.

P.P.S. Sorry about the crabbed handwriting. Too many days squeezing secateurs (not a euphemism).

★

To: Hugo Pickthorn, Victoria Beazley
Subject: Andy's resignation

Dear Hugo and Victoria,

I must confess my dismay, not only at Andy's resignation from the board, but at the language he used to announce it. His absurd allegations concerning Dr Surfleet and myself I am prepared to overlook, but his maligning of the good doctor was outrageous, given the kindness that our late friend showed when he bought Andy's smallholding. Naturally, I do not wish to cast aspersions, but it cannot be a coincidence that Andy and Mark Surfleet can regularly be seen together propping up the bar at The Queen's Oak.

Well, the Trust's work must continue. I look forward to continuing with the two of you in the years ahead.

Yours as ever,

Marjorie

★

Peebles, 9th October

Dear Connie,

Thanks for your letter. I'm *delighted* that you and Ella have decided to become parents! Mum would be so proud of you. I certainly am.

Compared with your news, mine is trivial. Redecoration at the farmhouse continues. You would approve of my fetish for Farrow & Ball. The trustees still distrust me. I had Vicky Beazley over for tea, attempting an intervention. It was all rather half-hearted on her part. I could see her scoping out the changes to Dad's decor. Half expected her to take a nostalgic glance at his bedroom, but she fought the urge and took tea with me in the orangery, where I explained my vision for Little Spinney. Colonel Pickthorn remains more circumspect. He's a dutiful old duffer, stands ramrod straight when we meet – at attention – though I know his heart is in bad shape and he pants when we make our way about the garden.

My chief antagonist remains Marjorie T. I doubt she has much else to do with her time. She's the kind of woman who writes birthday cards to herself addressed from her cat.

I wonder if there's a romantic dimension to her obsession. It is possible, isn't it, that Dad in his dotage had to lower his erotic standards. Who's to say he didn't settle for that horse's arse?

Ouch – just slapped my wrist on your behalf.

Sorry for the short letter. I just wanted to write "Whoopee!" at the prospect of becoming an uncle.

Love to you, Ella, and the zygote.

M xx

★

Contact Us Form

YOUR DETAILS

Title*	Ms
First Name*	Marjorie
Last Name*	Truscott
Email*	M.Truscott@yahoo.co.uk
Address Line 1*	Cherry Tree Cottage
Address Line 2	Longwater Lane
Address Line 3	Finchampstead
Postcode*	RG40 4NX

Are you a subscriber to The Daily Telegraph and Sunday Telegraph newspapers?	Yes X
	No

YOUR ENQUIRY

What does your enquiry relate to?*	Other

I have a story – rather a scoop – about a garden, open to the public and in the NGS Yellow Book, which is under threat from a vengeful inheritor. I wish to write in greater depth to your gardening correspondent Ken Godfrey, whom I believe knew the garden's creator. I would greatly appreciate it if you could pass this message on.

*

To: Nick Haggerty
Subject: Season of lists

Hi Nick,

Please find attached a hefty list of bulbs, saplings and seeds for winter. It's going to be a busy planting season! Hope you approve of the apple and pear varieties – worthy replacements for the ornamental cherries and their meretricious blossoms.

I'm sorry that Marjorie Truscott has been harassing you about supplying Little Spinney. I have told her that Dad's old stockist was overcharging, but to no effect. She views every innovation as a betrayal.

Best, as ever, to you and H.

Mark

*

To: Hugo Pickthorn, Victoria Beazley
BC: k.godfrey@telegraph.co.uk
Subject: Urgent

Dear Hugo and Victoria,

It seems our efforts to rescue the paths through the canal and sundial gardens have failed. Both have now been shut off with fencing and hedgerow saplings quite inappropriately planted to justify the enclosure. I have also discovered that, despite assurances, work has begun to brick up the view of the farmhouse from the rill garden. These developments are as nothing, however, to my final discovery. Tom Atkins had warned me of plans to replace the ornamental cherries, but nothing could have prepared me for the shock of finding the entire avenue destroyed. I telephoned M.S. to protest and his only response was that 'the trees will be replaced'. Yes, but they will not be Gerald's trees!

I understand that you have attempted individually to reason with M.S. He can be a very persuasive and charming young man when it suits him. I have little doubt that he is endeavouring to break up the Trust, and to rid himself of all hindrances to his ambitions for Little Spinney. We must not let him succeed.

I would appreciate it if you could respond to this email as quickly as possible.

Marjorie

*

To: Marjorie Truscott
CC: little-spinney-trustees@googlegroups.com
Subject: Under investigation

Dear Marjorie,

I know that we do not agree on all aspects of gardening. I regret that I spoke harshly to you on the telephone. Neither of these things justifies your subjecting me to investigation by a journalist. You will appreciate that it came as something of a surprise to find one trespassing on my driveway. What followed I can only describe as an interrogation. He said you accused me of 'infesting' Little Spinney with bees. Of course I regret what happened to your niece, but such is nature. Surely, as a gardener, you must recognise the vital role played by pollinators. As for the other accusations, I shan't bother to list them all, but I will tell you this: if my sister and I have any interest or expertise in gardening, it is entirely the result of our mother's example and not our father's. Finally, let me assure you that I have not 'hounded' Tom out of Little Spinney. The man is perfectly entitled to his retirement. I will of course miss his help and expertise, but with conservation volunteers stepping in at the weekends, I am confident we will be able to manage the land.

Yours, *etc.*
Mark Surfleet

*

To: Victoria Beazley
BC: k.godfrey@telegraph.co.uk
Subject: Duplicity

Dear Victoria,

I resent your suggestion that I am being paranoid. Before his death, Gerald confided in me about his ex-wife and her manipulative ways. Heda was quite capable of appearing the victim of an injustice when she was its perpetrator: she was, after all, an actress. It seems plausible that these tendencies were passed on to her children. Given that M.S. inherited his father's charm, why should he not also have inherited his mother's duplicity?

Yours as ever,

Marjorie

*

Dear Vicky – hope you like the postcard – one of the tamer ones from Dad's collection. I should be delighted to have dinner with you: thank you for the invitation. Shall I bring some apples from the orchard? We've a glut of Egremont Russets. Best wishes – Mark

*

Cherry Tree Cottage, 18th November

Dear Hugo,

Thank you for your email. I have nothing to say about Victoria Beazley. You seem to consider her resignation a disaster. I, on the other hand, see it as an opportunity to close ranks and redouble our efforts.

I did indeed contact *The Telegraph*. I make no apologies, when M.S. is walling up views and stretching out barbed wire.

Is he preparing for a siege?

It is still possible to save Little Spinney. I cannot pretend to be disinterested. Gerald meant to share his garden with the world, yet his son, who boasts of his progressive views, wishes to turn it into a private wilderness. Little Spinney is not the repository of his memories only. In the years of my parents' final illnesses, walking its paths and charting its development was my only solace.

I remain your friend and fellow trustee,

Marjorie

★

Little Spinney, 21st November

Dear Connie,

As you can see, I am back in Berkshire. Peebles was lovely – great to see some of the old gang – but I feel my life is here now. We've had our first frost and I'm making use of a mild weekend to plant out daffodil bulbs. It seems ironic that Dad, of all people, should have been indifferent to *Narcissi*.

Did I tell you that Vicky Beazley has resigned? It's hardly a surprise. Sitting down with another of Dad's old flames must have made her feel past it, poor thing. Marjorie T. is still on the warpath. Now she has Ken Godfrey on my case. Claims he used to play golf with Dad at Wentworth. A frightful snob and something of a lush. We should prepare ourselves for a public drubbing. We are, after all, ungrateful children. There seems little point explaining that Dad conceived his garden with more love than went into our making.

I had a phone call this evening from Colonel Pickthorn. Seems his wife is very ill – a stroke. He sounded shaken up, the poor old boy. I suggested he take a break from his duties as chair of the Trust. I hope he does.

To end on a cheerier note, I look forward to hearing about

your first scan! I hope it goes well. In the meantime, picture me in the hollowed out library, sitting before the seed catalogue, about to turn my mind to the delectable task of beginning afresh.

M x

Bottleneck

A FOOT ON HER bladder jolts her awake. She queues for the toilet, is ushered to the front by kindly passengers, and on returning to her seat discovers East Anglia overlaid with a map of vapour. She pretends to herself that this is stable English cloud, its blue lacunae the Norfolk Broads that she has never visited. The thought makes her thirsty and, looking down the aisle for the drinks trolley, she reaches into her purse for change. She requests a tomato juice and watches as the hostess measures out a sample. She takes a sip and her taste buds seem to revive like flowers after rain. Taking her time with the dregs, she sits back to consider all that has taken place — the journey to and from Berlin, her courtesy tour of the heat-dazed city, the performance at the Konzerthaus. Is it common for the Small Hall to have so many empty seats? No matter: the applause sounded genuine and lasted a long time, until she began to suspect that it was her condition, rather than her composition, that won people over; for she had been summoned to the front of the stage and exposed there, bashful, elated and flagrantly pregnant, until the first violin encumbered her with a bouquet and turned her into an allegorical figure from a masque of plenty.

There is a second jolt. Passengers murmur as the plane lurches through fathoms of air. Clare grips the armrest and shuts her eyes. She reminds herself of the statistics about aircraft safety. All the same, she does not open her eyes or wipe the perspiration from her upper lip until they are safely delivered from turbulence.

'Now that was a drop,' her neighbour says. 'Cheaper to stay at home and fall down the stairs.'

Clare nods and sketches a smile. She resists the urge ethically to justify her presence on board, to describe to this affluent woman the difficulties of securing a permit, the cost of exceeding her carbon allowance and her worries about the ethics of doing so.

Ajay insisted that she go. Hasn't she always told him that Germany values new music, whereas in England only the comforting oldies have an audience: the vanished pastoral of Elgar and Vaughan Williams. Clare's compositions, swarming with terror and magnificence, hold scant appeal to such patrons as remain to fill the void left by public subsidy. Who wants orchestral noise that frightens and dismays? Berliners, it would seem. They absorbed, as if they deserved it, the stern sermon of her *Threnody* and meditated on it afterwards in the air-conditioned café. The balm of their approval was soured for Clare by a few sidelong glances at her fullness, from abstainers perhaps, or else music enthusiasts who foresaw, as she does, with a pang of apprehension, the sinking of her gifts under nappies and night feeds.

She rests her hands on her belly. Her lower back aches; her bladder seems full again. She feels gross, usurped — time to be done with it all. Yet she fears the pain of labour and has complained to Ajay about the ordeal ahead. Having to squeeze a living body through that tearing, agonised neck.

'Men have it easy. All the fun and none of the effort.'

'What about gallstones?'

'I think you'll find a baby is a bit bigger.'

'A baby passes through a bigger aperture.'

'Oh God — can't I just pay someone to do it for me? If men had to do this you'd have come up with a technofix years ago.'

'There are some things, my love, that cannot be fixed by technology.'

The aircraft dips towards England. Clare sees through the window the cloud dissolve to reveal the faded quilt of Essex, the fields and woods from this height a blend of coffee and cream, with here and there the glint, like dropped shreds of foil, of solar panels on domestic roofs. The plane tilts again to reveal the vast circuitry of London smudged by photochemical smog.

'Beautiful,' her neighbour says, leaning close to see out. Clare inhales the woman's perfume and mutters about pollution. 'I don't think so,' says the woman. 'That's just humidity, isn't it?'

Clare warns herself not to take against this frequent flyer with her Botoxed brow, her snakeskin handbag and farded cheeks. Above all, do not get polemical. It is a side to her nature that has not served her well. In Germany, it was better received. She was able to describe, without inwardly cringing, the subject of her *Threnody*, a funeral piece for the non-human Earth to which, now that we have despoiled it, we have no option but to pay attention. Ideally, her music would embody its purpose, yet whenever a journalist calls, she finds the urge to proselytise difficult to resist. It has made her enemies — like Quentin Barber in *The Telegraph*, who claimed to have discovered in her song cycle, *The Sleep of Reason*, 'an ideological focus reminiscent of the vanished commissars of socialist realism'.

The seatbelt sign lights up, the captain gives his instructions, and the plane bucks and trembles into its final descent. Maybe she does hector; maybe she is a bore. Only second-rate composers write programmatically. Yet the state of things drives her to it. How can she keep silent? Clare envies Ajay his philosophical calm. The Earth will shrug us off, he says, if it has to. Life won't end with humans. Sometimes his fatalism infuriates her, is endurable only with the knowledge that rather than wailing at the crisis he is acting to resolve it; whereas she obsesses at the news of famines in Africa and Southeast Asia, and scrabbles around for ways to make sense of it all in music that, to most ears, is nothing but discordant noise.

The plane lands without complications, and Clare leans under the thin ventilation jet to dispel her nausea. Already the woman beside her is gathering her things. Clare waits with eyes closed for the plane to taxi and dock. Perhaps, she tells herself, the birth will change everything, narrowing her focus to daily necessities. It might be a relief to have one person's future to worry about above all others: a fraction of the world it is in her power to protect.

Ajay is waiting at the arrivals gate. The stubble is dark on his face; he looks tired. He runs his hand over The Bump before giving her a quick, dry kiss.

'We're not taking the Tube in this heat. I've got a car.'

Clare lets him take the lead. They are exposed briefly to the blast of the day before entering the multi-storey car park. With what feels like almost terminal lassitude, she eases herself into the passenger seat of the hired vehicle. It smells of new upholstery and sun-baked plastic. A previous user has stuffed the glove compartment with used wet wipes.

Ajay negotiates the twists of the car park, the wheels making a high lament at every turn. He steers them past checkpoints and through bollards into broiling traffic.

'I'm sorry,' says Clare.

'For what?'

'For not being talkative. It's nothing personal.'

She contemplates the sunlight caught in the hairs of his forearm. She prefers not to look at the countryside. Better to burrow into her thoughts and contemplate the man she loves.

The first she knew of Ajay was his voice – followed by his hands, lithe and articulate like his speech, fluttering half a dozen panellists from where she sat onstage at the FutureScope conference. She leaned forward, to the edge of inelegance, until she could connect that wry baritone, those elegant hands, to their owner. The face was not handsome (the eyes fractionally prominent, the chin distinctly receding) yet resting her gaze on it felt like a homecoming. It was not so much a sensation of déjà vu as of stepping back into a foundational element, the first air of childhood, when everything is remarkable. She *liked* this man with his baffling talk of recyclable coenzymes and photoautotrophic organisms. There was something Promethean about his ambition to reveal one of the great mysteries of life on Earth: life which had created the conditions for more of itself. Watching him talk, she could not help smiling. Was he straight? Did he have a girl in the auditorium? And was this joy she felt illusory, a somatic defence against the talk of tipping points and feedback loops and vanished albedo effects?

After the plenary session, she made her way through the crowd and introduced herself. They shook hands and continued talking until they found themselves mirroring one another's postures on either side of a café table. Within a week, they were lovers; within three months, she had moved into his flat in Maida Hill. It was just possible to fit in her piano. When Ajay's startup received the backing of a VC firm in Shandong, they were able to rent a small semi within walking distance of Bayswater's gated communities. The area is reasonably secure and the house big enough for them to balance intimacy with the absorption of their respective callings.

Each endows the work of the other with the mystery of arcane secrets. Clare perceives as metaphor her partner's quest to store solar energy in the chemical bonds of a fuel, but she hears rather than listens to his talk of liquid catalysts and electrochemical cells, while Ajay sits proudly through church hall recitals of his wife's stringent and elusive music, all the while wondering, she supposes, what's for supper, or whether messages of interest are gathering on his phablet.

In the car, now, Ajay glances at the screen clipped to the dashboard. Clare presses back into the headrest in order to read it. Nothing but his Twitter feed.

'Are you following a news story?'

'Just chatter.' Ajay turns the screen off and Clare rests a hand on his knee.

'I hope you've been sleeping while I've been away.'

'When I get round to it.'

'Seriously, you look tired.'

'I'm in training.'

'You'd be better off building up reserves.'

'For the Sleep Crunch.' A panic of sirens blazes its way through the traffic. 'It's good to have you back.'

'It's good to be back.'

Ajay, emboldened by this exchange, begins to ask detailed questions about her flight, how it felt to be doing something to which they had once been accustomed. Does Clare imagine it, or is there a forced quality to his inquiries? The heat, the flight, the long queues at security and to get her rations deducted, have left her jangled. As gently as she can, she asks Ajay for quiet, and spends the rest of the journey with her eyes closed, in part to keep from seeing outside, in part to find in herself some point of calm.

The sun has passed its zenith by the time he has dropped her off, gone to park the car in its charging bay and come home to find her sitting in the kitchen, tights in hand, curling and uncurling her swollen toes. She hands him the twin of her sweating glass.

'London's finest,' she says. 'Recycled a thousand times.'

'All water's recycled.' They drain their glasses and Ajay gasps in that theatrical way that niggles at her. 'What's up?'

'Huh?'

'You seem preoccupied.'

'Of course I'm preoccupied. Look at the size of me!'

She contemplates her splayed toes on the linoleum floor and does not look up until Ajay has left the room with her suitcase. She levers herself to her feet and begins to drift about the house, as if reacquainting herself with a place long ago abandoned. In the bedroom, she takes off her blouse and contemplates her belly: a pale globe with a line of longitude bisecting the navel. Something sits, an obstruction, in her stomach. The feeling has accumulated like thunder in the heat until, in a sudden revelation while she unpacks her suitcase, it cascades into a six-bar motif: a tremulous murmur in the strings, an embryonic pulse from bassoon and oboe, and then a solitary French horn launching on C major, only to lose faith in itself and slide back with a melancholy glissando.

She makes her way to the piano and scribbles it down: the sketch of her theme. The seed of the work that was germinating inside her.

She hears movement in the garden and look out to see Ajay plucking dead stems from the soft fruit. She barely notices the parched condition of the laurels, the grass like straw, the leaves of the dwarf apple puckered and jaundiced. She attends to her breathing. The mind must lie still and open like the palm of a hand. Whatever comes must not be rushed. To reach for it is to chase it away.

She looks at the notes hung out on the staff paper. She tries them again, her ear casting a line beyond the last reverberation. Drops of sweat fall on the piano keys. She hears as if on a wandering breeze the stridulation of violins, feverish rumbles from a full complement of doubles basses. Twisting over both, like butterflies in a pheromonal dance, oboe and bassoon restate and interrogate the opening theme. These forces – the elemental strings, the creaturely wind – are in opposition, and her body aches with the tension. She writes the parts one above another, forcing herself to concentrate. It's like hauling herself rung by rung along a horizontal ladder. The weight is too much to carry. She lets go and turns on the piano stool to face the room: its books and scores, its row upon row of antiquated CDs.

Clare hears Ajay come inside and go to his study, closing the door behind him. She dares another look at the sketches and wonders what kind of music can welcome a child into a world of ashes. Will their daughter live to witness a miraculous

escape from the bottleneck in which humanity is now horribly
wedged? Or will she – the question terrifies – be among the
millions to die in its breathless confinement?

The analogy belongs to a science blogger: their friend Olive.
'Here we are,' she said that time after supper, 'the buffers hit years
ago – peak phosphate, peak water, peak everything – and the
chemical structure of the atmosphere altered beyond recovery.
We have squeezed ourselves into this bottleneck. Either we get
smart or history ends this century.' This talk terrified Clare. She
made an excuse and hurried to the bathroom, her heart
pounding. Olive's words called to mind the mouse she
discovered once, jammed inside a wine bottle discarded under
their hedge: killed for the sweetness that lured it in.

Clare gathers herself off the stool. For the umpteenth time
today, she goes to the toilet to ease the pressure on her bladder.
Reaching for a square of paper, she wonders if, under the
surface, Ajay too isn't panicked by what is about to descend on
them. Quite apart from the ecological questions – the world
has no need of another human – is it right to forge a
consciousness that must suffer and die? There are those who
say we have a duty to *resist* our biology. Ten years ago, they
were the ones telling us to stop shopping, to break our
addiction to growth for the future's sake. Yet the bulk of
humanity heeds old imperatives. We let nature takes its course
– even if nature's course is, ultimately, to purge itself of us.

Clare told very few people about her pregnancy while it
was still possible to conceal it. She dreaded disapproval; yet no
one, not even Tilda who runs a despair management course at
the university, displayed anything other than delight at the
prospect once it was obvious. In the abstract, people with
whom Clare and Ajay socialise parade their scepticism about
breeding, but when it comes to their own lives, or those of
friends, the opposition fades. The impulse is too strong, it's a
compulsion pushed on us like a drug by our genes. The baby
wants to be born – isn't that the truth? It announced itself,
circumvented their precautions, technology no match for that

lone swimmer and her porous, eager egg.

She knocks on the door of Ajay's study and goes in to kiss him on the crown of his head. Half a dozen tabs are open on his monitor: emails, news items, syndicated feeds on air pollution and the riots. She wraps her arms about his damp shoulders.

'What would you say, Mr Four-Eyes, to some supper?'

Ajay rests a hand on her forearm but does not return her playful tone. 'Are you up to it?'

'I think I can manage something simple.'

In the kitchen, the floor is cool beneath her feet. She inspects the jars of pulses and quinoa, measures out the latter and puts a pan to boil. The fridge is full of drought-stunted vegetables. She tests the tomatoes, quarters them; dices spring onions and radishes. It pleases her to cook when they have fresh produce. Nutri-shakes and algal compounds may be necessary but she cannot find in their preparation the sacramental quiet she looks for in domestic tasks. Every action must be undertaken with reverence. How hateful to be on autopilot, never to wake fully into the day.

Half an hour later, with a breeze at last creeping in from the garden, she lays the quinoa salad on the table. Ajay joins her in silence but it takes her several minutes, caught up in the undertow of her music, to notice his hunched shoulders and the slowness with which he lifts the fork to his lips. She looks at him, hoping to draw his attention with her eyes. His own are hooded and he keeps his head bowed over the plate. Only when they have eaten and Ajay takes their plates to the sink does she ask what is troubling him.

'I don't know if it matters,' he says.

'If what matters?'

'In the grand scheme of things.'

'Ajay.'

'Come upstairs. It would be easier to show you.'

She follows him, her stomach aflutter, into his study, where he wakes the computer with a flick of the mouse. Clare's eyes wander, too weary to settle, over emails and campaign pages and various business sites. 'What am I looking for?'

'PhotoGen,' says Ajay, 'has been neutered.'

'What do you mean?'

'See for yourself.'

Clare leans forward and tries to narrow in on a single paragraph. She sees familiar names and acronyms. Dread parches her mouth. 'For God's sake, tell me what's happened.'

'Shall I bullet point it for you?'

'No, just tell me outright.'

Ajay hesitates and she has to master her frustration at being toyed with, at having to wait for an explanation. 'The mistake we made was to think we could play with the big boys...'

Clare stares at him. She recalls Ajay's reluctance to tangle even with the remotest tentacles of that vast energy empire.

'They have decided...' Ajay sighs, and she can hear the effort in his voice to keep calm. '...to cease investing in uncertain technologies in order to focus on proven energy. For which read tar sands and coal-to-oil. Remote extraction in the Arctic.'

'You said they gave assurances.'

'They made all the right noises. We thought we were taking good advice, but who's to say the advice wasn't paid for by someone else?'

'So who owns the largest share?'

'*They* do, Clare. It was their game plan all along: get a foothold and then take over.'

'How's it in their interest to shut you down?'

'It's entirely in their interests, if you think in quarterlies. Look, there's nothing new in their MO. You buy technology that threatens you and you suffocate it. Like a heroin dealer stealing the city's supply of methadone and burning it.'

'Why didn't you *tell* me?'

'You were in Berlin. I didn't want to spoil your concert. Then this afternoon you looked tired...'

'Just when I'd started –' Clare wavers and Ajay, reproaching himself for his inattention, eases her onto the office chair. She has to swivel away from the screen – cannot bear to see those urgent tabs with their freight of bad news. 'I've started something new.'

'Can't hear you, love.'

'I'm thirsty,' she says.

He rushes downstairs while Clare leans forward, her pregnancy vast between her thighs. Ajay returns with a glass of water and watches her drink.

'Are you...?' She tries to find a way out, an escape clause however tenuous. 'Is it certain they're going to defund you?'

'Andy and Neil have been texting me all day. That's the rumour. And there's no going elsewhere when they own the patents.' Ajay leans against the bookcase and folds up till he is kneeling before her, like a supplicant at the altar of his child. 'I wanted to believe in the possibility of good faith. Their money and our forward-thinking. Proof that even the most entrenched interests can see where the future lies. The irony is, they can. They see where we're heading, which is why they've spent decades trying to stop us from getting there.'

Clare runs her fingers through his hair, careful not to touch his bald patch. She sees a little boy in need of saving. How can she console him, she who has always needed his stability, his resistance to hope or despair? That dinner party, seated between technological optimists and depletionist Olive, he had argued against both contentions. She has seen him refute, gently but without evasion, activists clinging to the dream that resource depletion will bring down the ogre of industrial capitalism. Ah, he'd say, but that fails to reckon with its resourcefulness. The last acre of Earth will have been scoured before the system admits its madness. Perhaps, then, the giant will fall, but it will fall on the people below. Our task, the task of innovators, is to keep the giant on its feet and make it move more daintily until it learns a different dance.

Another thought, closer to home, pushes these metaphors aside. How will they manage with a baby on the way? She asks him the question.

'Oh, any settlement will be generous,' he says. 'I can probably find work with another start-up. Don't worry on that score.'

The word brings her back to herself. She hears a mockery of trumpets, flatulent brass: a tide of noise drowning the tentative music of Earth. Too obvious? Yet the obvious is what we fail to take note of. She listens for the next wave of sound. The next iteration.

'We're out of time anyway,' says Ajay. 'It was too late ten years ago. We've been looking for a technofix but it's our minds we have to change not our means. And there's no app for improving human nature.'

Clare turns, reaching for the windowsill. She stands on solid floorboards yet feels the world falling away. Into dread. Towards chaos. The chthonic darkness. Then a lone violin, unnoticed at first, forcing its way through the noise like a weed through concrete. She listens for it. Desperately.

'I thought denial was a failing in others. And all this time I've been at the bargaining stage.'

The melody, thin and fragile, begins to spread like a virus to the other strings.

'I'm sorry...' says Clare. She makes her way, cradling the music in her thoughts, to the piano. He follows her and leans against the door jamb, watching.

'It arrived this afternoon,' she says without looking up. 'While you were in the garden. I can't just let it pass.'

'You don't imagine anyone's ever going to perform it, do you?'

She writes, then puts down her pencil on the score rest and contemplates the vacant doorway. Downstairs, the fridge door opens and a bottle top dances on the granite counter.

Clare looks at the scrawl of her notation. She sounds the emptiness in her core – sorrow's anaesthetic. She hears Ajay open the door to the garden and the respite of darkness.

Perhaps she has always known. To live, as one must, day to day, is to depend on saving illusions. Saving, that is, until they drown us. She breathes slowly. The air is kind to life. Life made it, after all. She must not give herself to anger or sorrow. The score is growing inside her. It will not save one life, yet with it she will add to the store of creation.

She thinks of Ajay standing among the withered beds. In a minute, she will go to him. First, she looks at the score: that scrawled clef, those crochets and minims. What else can she do with the time that remains?

Their child is coming into the world.

Nothing can stop it now.

The Modification of Eugene Berenger

To: Erlking, Goldie, Leopardgurrl, Horny Bob.
From: Fr. Terence Mode

Greetings — as the priest of an old faith might have begun a letter to colleagues in the world gone by. It's status orange here in San Francisco, the storm belts having passed with only minimal damage, and the Seminary exudes a sense of purpose as we await the arrival of a fresh intake. I imagine it must seem a long time since the beginning of your novitiates, yet to me the process of renewal is like the seasons of old, a cycle of change which embodies the mystery of regeneration. I look forward to encountering new and startling permutations: the diversity of forms which only the young seem capable of. Yet I confess to some trepidation, for the mind seeks what is known and established, and even those of us who belong to the pioneering generation crave, as we get older, a kind of stasis, a settling into established norms, so that we can travel without further dislocation to the final transformation of death.

It is difficult to be a student of flux. We set our hearts against change, we long to be frozen when everything flows. Yet I have witnessed the thaw many times, and wish to share one instance with you. It is a story of resistance and needless pain. It concerns my old university friend, Eugene Berenger, and his attempt to swim against the tide of the world. My role in the story is small but significant: that of a conduit, tasked with advancing the plot to its only possible conclusion. Sometimes that is all we are called upon to do. We are ferrymen, my brothers and sisters. We are guides leading the blind to the fountain of sight.

I had known Eugene Berenger, on and off, for fifty years, ever since our young days sheltering from the Great Recession in the groves of academe. Our friendship had waxed and waned over the decades, but when I received his email last year it had dwindled thinner than a crescent moon. I had, however, gotten to know his wife, Marie, after she came to seek my guidance on her path to Eclosion. The joy of her conversion had reconciled her to their daughter, Sally, whereupon Eugene moved out of the marital home to a one-bedroom apartment in Portola. He informed me of this himself, in an email full of intemperate exclamations. He would remain true to himself, he wrote, even at the expense of family and friends. I recognised at once the symptoms. We must think of them not as faults but as patterns, neither to be dismissed nor condemned but alleviated with care. For compassion is our watchword: the liberation of imprisoned forms must be done tenderly, using all the tools of science and revelation.

Troubled by his email, I decided to pay Eugene a visit. I wasn't sure what state I would find him in. Even when we were freshmen I had noticed the morbid cast of his thoughts. He used to obsess about his grades and would gnaw like a dog at the bone of some grievance: the sarcasm of a tutor or the scorn of a beautiful classmate. We headed, after Berkeley, in different directions – me towards the sacraments, he into the dusty and, being done, reassuring obscurity of European history. The past and its memories were a place of safety for him, as they remain for many of my contemporaries. Your generation, of course, has never had the luxury of nostalgia.

Eugene Berenger was surviving in a squalid apartment block on Burrows Street, where I arrived by cab and searched for his number. He buzzed me in and, after refusing my hand, which he regarded with undisguised horror, admitted me to a disordered room that smelled of pizza and olives. I could tell from the set-up that he had been sitting, before my arrival, among consoles that were streaming several newsfeeds at once. I thought of an addict gorging on what sickens him. (You will recall, from your training, that an unhealthy preoccupation with current affairs is a classic symptom of Aversion.) I looked about for evidence of previous visitors. There were no photographs of Marie or Sally, and I commented on the fact while he cleared a place for me to sit.

'I can't bear,' he said, 'to contemplate what I've lost.' He straightened to look at me and there was defiance in his eyes. 'I didn't think you'd come after what I wrote.'

'How could I not? Your email had the force of a summons.'

'Or a curse,' he said, and sat down amidst the dismal footage. 'Is Marie all right?'

'I've no idea. Why don't you ask her?'

He gave no reply, merely huffed sarcastically and muted the sound on the monitors.

'I'm sure she would appreciate hearing from you,' I said.

'Did she tell you that herself?' It was my turn to meet a question with silence. 'It all started with those experiments...'

'What did?'

'You know darned well. It's like,' he said, 'the old narcotics trade. The reversible stuff – those gels they put under their skin – that's the gateway drug. Get people used to looking like mutants and they'll move on to permanent upgrades. Like the ones – Christ, Terence, what if your mother could see you now?'

I laughed at this: it was such old world talk. 'My mother taught me to be true to myself.'

'By doing *that* to your face?'

My instinct to make light of this complaint faltered at the sight of tears in his eyes. 'Oh Eugene,' I said, 'there's no need to suffer.'

'I can't help it!'

'You're nostalgic for a world that's gone.'

'At Berkeley you were so good-looking I could hear people catch their breath when we walked into a room. I used to hang out with you just to be near all that promise. You seemed to embody the beauty of the world.'

'Well now everybody can. Think of it that way.'

'That isn't *beauty*. Beauty's natural. What you and your cultists do –'

'I can't accept that word.'

'– what you do is *wrong*. I don't care if I sound like I'm from Alabama or Utah: nothing will change my mind that body modification is a sin against nature.'

'I think we all know,' I said, 'about sins against nature. Mammon was the god of the *old* religion. Don't tar my Church with that brush.'

Eugene blew his nose and dabbed at his red-rimmed eyes. 'I'm sorry. It's just I take things hard. The loss of Sally... and now Marie...'

'They're not dead, Eugene.'

'Don't tell me I haven't lost them.'

'You haven't.'

'They're *gone*.'

'Only to Modesto. There's no reason to hurt yourself like this. To hurt them.'

I could have saved my breath. Eugene was not in a place to hear me. 'You know,' he said, 'she never told me who talked her into it. Who brainwashed her.'

'Why do you suppose it was brainwashing?'

'Oh, come on. This is my wife we're talking about. I *know* her.'

'Do you? Isn't it perhaps the discovery that she wasn't the person you thought she was –'

'She was kidnapped, okay? I don't mean literally but she was taken away from her life. They all are.'

'Was I?'

He faltered. 'You have a talent for sounding reasonable.' I

was careful not to soften the scrutiny of my gaze. 'Am I a bigot, Terence? Am I just some throwback – a reactionary who's outlived his time?'

'Your emotions are entirely understandable. The task is not to reproach yourself for them. It is to change them for the better.'

'I guess it must have been like this in Rome,' he said, 'when the Christ cult took over. The empire was dying and the old beliefs with it. People must have felt dislocated. They must have despaired.'

'Do you despair, Eugene?'

'You'd like that, wouldn't you? It would give you something to work with.'

I let him know, with a chromatic shift in my corneas, that I would not be unsettled by his hostility. He cleared his scrawny throat – so different from my own, though we are of an age.

'Maybe I'm getting old,' he said. 'I *am* old. So are you.'

'In body perhaps.'

'I guess when Sally did that to herself and Marie followed... I blamed you. I mean that it was your, uh, face that came to my mind. The face you used to have.'

'Which one?'

'That serene smile of yours. Like a Buddha. Beaming at the mutilation of those I love. Oh I know that word's taboo – it's an obscenity to describe an obscenity. But what else can you call the warping of a woman's natural body?'

'We call it Eclosion. Like the emergence of a butterfly from its chrysalis.'

'I call it a flight from reality.'

'We're not escaping reality, we're outflanking it.'

'But changing our bodies like this, altering our nature. It's a failure of solidarity with the past.'

'The past failed in its solidarity with the future. Why should we be nostalgic for a place that made us homeless?'

Eugene was not easily to be persuaded. Morphing, he said, is the result of human arrogance. Our bodies having evolved over millions of years, who are we to promote ourselves above all other life?

'That, if I may say so, is a classic misapprehension. You must have noticed the forms we take – the sources of our inspiration. By embodying our kinship with other species, we have not dethroned humanity so much as democratised creation.' I reminded him how Morphers across the globe have made their bodies living memorials to the species which our forbears extinguished: the Rhino Boys of Botswana, Pandaoists in China, the clawed and banded women haunting the ruins of Ranthambore in homage to the tigers that used to roam there. Eugene seemed affected by these instances: I could see him grimace as he fought to tamp down something in his chest. I asked if he would take some water but he shook his head.

'How many of the freaks you mention,' he said, 'have corporate sponsors? And don't think I won't see you lying. I know about your corneal implants.'

'I have no reason to lie to you, Eugene. The Church is consistent on the matter. We oppose the commercialisation of Morphing – commerce being the lifeblood of the domination system.' I reminded him how that system had revealed its true nature in the enhancement scandals that brought down the Olympics.

'And how!' he said. 'I never could figure out how you guys survived that shit storm. Of course you blamed commerce for hijacking something beautiful.'

'Body dissatisfaction had always been a weapon in advertising's arsenal. It was the most obvious step in the world to link morphing to fashion, body modification to consumerism. For corporations it was like pushing an open door. The new generation, raised by virtual moms and housebots, inured themselves to norms that meant little to them. By adolescence, daily immersion in the Pornstream ensured that a young person felt out of the ordinary, was frankly something of a freak, not to possess at least a basic Dejina or meatotomised cock. Cupid, you know, is a coercive cherub. If electrocleansing your pubis is what it takes to be admitted to love's feast, how many will choose to starve? If, by painless immersion, you can rid yourself of the taint of pigment, why would you remain in darkness?'

'And you *approve* of this?'

'On the contrary! The repression of melanin is a deplorable phenomenon. It's conformism of the worst kind. The Church goes in the opposite direction: away from homogenisation into diversity, with many colours added to the few naturally available to us. You'll find no gene silencers in our hydrogels. We believe in a common process of revelation but in its individual manifestation.'

I watched Eugene consider these words. For a moment the weight seemed to lift from him. Perhaps it was the beginning of grace. I felt a door open, just a fraction, in his guarded soul, and reached out with a comforting hand. The movement was misjudged.

'Can't you see,' he cried, 'I don't care about these distinctions! I don't give a damn whether you're motivated by profit or prophecy – the net effect's the same. Morphing's what I object to, not the motivations behind it.' A sob escaped from his throat. 'It took my wife away from me. It took my baby girl. Everyone I love.'

He stood up, jolting the monitors, and staggered to the bathroom where I heard him heave and gasp. I hesitated, wondering whether I oughtn't to go to him, but I figured he would hate me for seeing him in his distress. There was a flush from the air cleanser and he returned, pale with determination.

'I think you should leave,' he said. 'I wrote because I wanted to see you – to witness what you'd done to yourself. I needed a good laugh.'

'Did I provide one?'

'Maybe you think I'm crazy to hold out alone. I wanted you to see me refuse what no one else can resist.'

'You speak to me as if I were your enemy.'

'Are you not?'

I got up to leave, but the pressure of his gaze goaded me to a candour that may have been incautious. 'I don't think you're crazy,' I said. 'I believe your soul is in torment for resisting what it most longs for.'

I left the apartment with his curses ringing in my ears.

And that might have been the last I saw of Eugene Berenger. I had not succeeded in helping him; if anything, I told myself as I returned to the seminary, I had turned away from one in Aversion. Yet I felt disinclined to start over, in view of what had passed. Little did I know that the working of grace had not yet finished with my old friend.

Two weeks after our encounter in Portola, I was meditating in my office when Father Funhouse announced on the intercom that an acquaintance of mine was being shown to my door. I opened the same a fraction of a second before my visitor knocked. Perhaps it was merely surprise that left his fist trembling in space a foot from my heart.

'You look exhausted,' I said, as I in my turn cleared a place for him to sit. He declined to take it. 'Have you spoken to your wife since we met? To your daughter?'

'Oh, you'd like that. That would fit your plan.'

He was trembling in all his extremities. I asked if he would care for a toke.

'God knows I've tried, I really have, to understand why they did it. To look at them without wanting to throw up. But I can't turn my mental world upside down. I can't reject what is scientifically normal.'

'Science has changed,' I said, sitting down to take some of the tension out of the air. 'It serves *us* now. For centuries, science gave us means at the expense of meaning. Once upon a time we were made in God's image, with the cosmos revolving around us. Now we're denizens of a rock in space, spinning on its axis towards extinction. This demotion made us mad. We plundered the Earth's resources to plug the meaning gap; we buried ourselves in a mausoleum of stuff, until we could no longer bear the daylight that revealed us to ourselves. The biosphere, it turned out, was our only source of meaning. And look what we'd done to it.'

'Denatured it,' said Eugene, 'like you want to denature me.'

'The Church wants nothing of the sort. We're not monsters.'

'Oh no – what would you call *that*?' He pointed at the picture of Father Ghoulish on my desk.

'You know I was speaking metaphorically.'

Eugene folded his arms across his chest to quell their shaking. I pretended not to notice. 'Historically,' I said, 'the forces of coercion worked the other way. Abstainers forget the prejudices we had to overcome before we went mainstream. There was resistance everywhere. A mermaid was drowned in Nantucket. Lizard boys were lynched in Tennessee. But we stood firm, convinced of our legitimacy. And we helped to transform medicine on the way. For example, tracheal implants used to feel to a lot of patients like an invasion, a mutilation. As lifestyle morphing became common, the mental stigma attached to medical procedures faded away. The shame went. The fear abated.'

'You pretend to love humanity – you talk all peace and love. But how can you love something when you want to alter it out of all recognition?'

'Elevate,' I said. I reminded him about our Foundational Creed: the fruit of our deliberations, that terrible hurricane year when everything changed. As the world altered, warping faster than our hearts and minds could adapt, we came to feel that the only way of reaching an accommodation with change was to run ahead of it, to make an adventure of transformation, to inscribe as it were on our flesh the startling dynamics of the Anthropocene. We bent science to a new and spiritual purpose. We used its discoveries to discover our potential. We became alchemists of the flesh, every Morpher his or her self-creation.

'That sounds like pride,' said Eugene.

'Not in the sense you intend. We don't worship ourselves.

That would be anthropolatry.'

'Gesundheit!'

'We morph in order to transcend the self, to escape, at first in form and thereby in spirit, the egocentricity that led our species to this unhappy pass.'

Eugene was not really listening. Like a man bent over a conundrum, or sounding in himself the first murmurs of a gastric complaint, he stood by the window viewing the sidewalk.

'Are you sure,' I said, 'I can't persuade you to sit? You're setting me on edge, standing like that.'

'I think I'm done with sitting.' Eugene pulled a folded sheet of paper from his pants and tossed it across my desk. I took it up and read the contents. I put the paper down.

'I hope you know we would never endorse this.'

'No you wouldn't. But you're the high priests of a tribe. And tribes need enemies to cement their identity. They need outsiders, non-members. People like me.'

'That,' I said, 'is a deplorable document. You should take it to the police.'

'You think they give a shit about Abstainers like me? For all I know, it was a cop who put that in my mailbox.'

I tried to assure him that this was wide of the mark. I offered to take up the matter myself, with the DA if necessary.

'The DA,' Eugene laughed. 'That bastard speaks with a forked tongue.'

'He can't very well help that.'

'Nobody can protect me. Nobody would even *want* to.'

'I want to help you, Eugene.'

'You? You're the original freak police. How could I turn to you for help when you're my enemy?'

'Please. How can you call me that after all these years?'

'It was you who advised my wife.'

My desk was really most extraordinarily dusty. 'Excuse me?' I said.

'You were her rabbi – confessor – whatever the heck you call it.'

'To my knowledge,' I said slowly, 'Marie and Sally came to Eclosion after making up their own minds.'

'You brainwashed them.'

'I did not.'

'You helped them fuck themselves up.'

'I had – absolutely and categorically – no part in fucking them up.'

Eugene shook his head. 'Wrong answer,' he said, and it took me a moment to recognize the revolver for what it was. The air drained from the room. My hands lifted of their own accord. That deadly aperture was all I could see, and it wasn't until he began pulling at the latch of the window that I guessed his intentions.

'What are you doing?'

'Enough with the lies. I'm letting some light in.'

'It's maximum UV out there. I don't think you should –'

'Hah!' he cried and, having released the latch, pulled up the windowpane. The heat blasted our bodies. I tried to get to him but the revolver kept me at bay. He waggled it a couple of times as he heaved a leg over the sill. My fingernails made contact for an instant with the belt of his pants. Two of them split to the quick with his momentum. I heard the impact of his body as it connected with the sidewalk. I was alone in my wind shaken room.

You will share with me, dear friends, my horror at what had come to pass. Yet I determined, in the days that followed Eugene Berenger's attempt on his life, not to let his suffering be in vain. As it was for my namesake, the Roman writer, nothing human is alien to me – not even an aversion so intense that it prefers annihilation to the transformation it so needlessly dreads. When Marie and Sally, now Tinkerbell, Berenger asked me to attend them at their loved one's bedside, I refused to allow the trauma of what I had witnessed to distract me from my duty.

The injuries sustained by Eugene were extensive: you will recall from your ordination how many flights up is my study.

It would be an indiscretion to share with you specific details of the damage done; suffice it to say that he had contrived, in his fall, to strike face-first the seminary railings. Eugene was put in an induced coma – would remain there for several weeks – and I endeavoured as best I could to console his wife and daughter. Marie Berenger, having power of attorney, was able, with my advice and blessings, to oversee the preliminary stages of reconstructive surgery that would ensure for Eugene a return to something resembling the life he had enjoyed.

Subcutaneous biosensors had been fitted, as a matter of course, on first admission to ER. The decision was then taken to fit an intrathoracic assist device that would pump oxygen to his damaged lungs. A nano-endoscope would allow his future carers to monitor his pathways. Nobody missed the irony that Eugene was being kept alive by the very technologies whose spiritual purpose he had so despised. Yet how could his loved ones have elected to replace a pulpy mess with the mere fleshly simulacrum of a nose when rhinoplastic alternatives are available that will not only replace but upgrade the usual functioning of the sense organ? It was not possible, even had it been desirable, to replace myopic, faded septuagenarian eyes with equally senescent grafts; what sense would there have been in trying, when UV-resistance comes as standard in the most basic ocular implants? The surgeons set to the task with their customary aplomb. And slowly, over weeks, Eugene Berenger returned to wakefulness. I ensured, after lengthy deliberations with hospital staff, that his resurfacing was managed at such a pace that Marie and I were able to introduce him gently to his altered condition. A shock at this early stage might have been fatal to him. His mental and somatic systems were protected by finely calibrated doses of morphine, anxiolytics and SSRIs. The decision was taken to control his serotonin receptor levels until such time as staff could be confident there would be no further attempt to act on his suicidal ideation.

We prayed over my old friend and wept, his wife and daughter and me, to see his resistance ebb away. He began not just to hear but to listen to us, and to see with eyes made new in both a literal and a metaphysical sense. He was equipped with an admirable set of new teeth. His auditory capacity was enhanced and the bone structure of his broken face extensively remodelled. It was a small step, in the end, to go from being reconciled to his palliative implants to embracing – as a Choice and a Way – the skeletal, muscular and dermal modifications which, his wife and I persuaded him, would make a virtue of medical necessity. 'There is nothing more sacred than life,' I reminded him while he moaned assent from beneath his plaster casts.

When the time came for Eugene's transfer from the ICU, I employed all my powers of persuasion, and called in favours going back to the earliest days of the Church, to secure a place for him at the Panta Rhei hospice up in Washington. I know what sterling work they do there to repair the links, so easily broken, between body and soul, life and hope, mere existence and spiritual joy.

You will note, my brothers and sisters, that the case of Eugene Berenger should not be taken as a practical instance of assisted transformation. It would be deplorable to steer an Abstainer towards self-harm in the hope of achieving what pure reason cannot. Instead, I share this story with you to illustrate not only the dangers of leaving a pathology untreated, but also by what extreme means fate, or what we properly call the Essence of Flux, may break through the hardest carapace to grant liberation to one who feared it. Having, in his obstinacy, left himself no other escape route, Eugene Berenger had to break himself and thereby break with the Inner Parent of his phobia. Despair and destruction allowed him, against the odds, to slough off the Exuvium of his old self – to emerge with iridescent wings from the chrysalis of denial. His Eclosion, for which daily his adoring wife and daughter give thanks, is a demonstration in extremis of transformational grace. For the news I receive on a regular basis from our colleagues at Panta Rhei is most encouraging. Only last week, he consented to the anointing of his brow with RNA-silencing chrism: thus wearing the first sign of his reconciliation to change – the bindi of the true Heraclitean flame.

Now I must leave you and clamber into my ceremonial robes. It is that happy time of year when I read the ordinal for missionaries passing out of my care, and receive into the same a fresh consignment of polymorphous beings. Accept, dear brothers and sisters in transfiguration, my loving salutations.

Terence

The Hermit of Athos

ON THE EDGE OF Holy Mountain, above the sea off Cape Akrothoos, there dwelt a Fool of God. Some thought his folly was feigned, others that it had driven him to this place of precipices, far from the solace of forests, to pursue the stillness and the silence that are the conditions of prayer.

Iakovos was the hermit's name. He had spent his early years at the monastery of Great Lavra, living as though fleshless, without a cell of his own, devoid of all possessions and sleeping only in the narthex of the church. In time, the voices of men became too loud for him and he took to the desert, where he lodged in caves, or sometimes a grass hut, above the plunge and spume of the cliffs. Clothed in a single garment, he would feed on acorns and plants in the woods about Great Lavra. Though he scorned the stimulation of human company, he accepted for survival's sake the monastery's gifts of rice and beans. And it was in the imagination of the bringer of this food – a young monk of unrecorded name – that Iakovos' unhappy fate took hold.

The young monk, who had not arrived at dispassion, surmised in the hermit a guide to spiritual eminence, and he carried his rations up the mountain in the hope of a few words of wisdom. But Iakovos, each time he heard the stranger approaching, would strip to his loincloth and stare like one distracted at the burning sky.

All summer and autumn this continued, the young man hungry for the hermit's vision. Then winter came, with its biting snow, its fangs of ice. Monks leaving the *katholikon* after Vespers found the young monk leaning at the well. He seemed exhausted from his climb. As they carried him inside, they heard him praising a divine light. He drank wine and whimpered as aged hands pressed life back into his feet. He was asked what he meant by this talk of light, and he answered, though racked by shivers:

'It came from Iakovos – from his hut – like a burning. I saw him stretch out his arms. And a flame of fire rose above his head. It reached as far as the branches of a tree. But the tree did not burn.' Monks gathered to hear the story. Some muttered against the hermit, others whispered his praises. 'I asked him,' continued the young man, "Father, what are you doing?' but he just looked through me as if I were the breeze.'

Father Kallistos was sceptical. 'Iakovos was ever an actor,' he said. 'His thirst for the divine is great. If it cannot be quenched, he will have us believe he is a Fool of God.'

There was a general murmur of agreement. The *geron* Theophanes, former spiritual guide to Iakovos and now, as securer of provisions, a man too weighed down by the duties of his office to empty himself through prayer, conceded that Iakovos feigned madness. 'But the false fool may act out of humility,' he said, 'to avoid praise and attention. I, for one, believe in the possibility of his transfiguration.'

With these words, the tide of opinion turned. Father Theodore, newly returned from eremitic life, claimed that he once saw Iakovos fly to the summit of the Holy Mountain – 'there to converse with our Theotokos, the beloved Mother of God.' Other monks, starved and brilliant-eyed, pressed forward with their accounts of the hermit's saintliness. They too had seen him levitate; they too had witnessed the heatless fire.

The young monk, his face burning, felt he was losing his advantage. 'The hermit sees into the future!' he cried. The monks were silenced; they bent to listen. 'A month ago, when I took him bread, Iakovos spoke to me. He prophesied the storm that brought down our cypress tree. He prophesied the raid by the Ishmaelites on Esphigmenou, and the sickness in Great Lavra that has robbed us of our three brothers.'

With this, declared the *geron*, the young monk had gone too far, and he was gently rebuked. Yet his words had flown into the world. They could not be gathered back.

The winter ground on, wind howling without and hunger within. Many hermits came to the monastery, perishing, from their *asceteria*. But Iakovos withstood all, flaying sun or burning snow. He was one of God's athletes. Even so, he must have rejoiced like other men at the return of spring.

With the swallows came the first pilgrims. Great need impelled them to the Holy Mountain, for many were the territories being conquered by the Ishmaelites. The pilgrims came for blessing and to beg God's mercy at the church of Great Lavra; and there, in conversation with the monks, they were acquainted with the presence, in the desert, of a holy fool and prophet. A few clambered up the cliff to see him. Iakovos, a near skeleton hung with tanned hide, set fire to his dwelling and sought stillness and silence further up the mountain.

The hermit's fame spread beyond Great Lavra. Pilgrims returning through Ouranoupolis carried it in their mouths: the flame of legend-to-be. Everywhere it found new kindling, across the windy mountains of Chaldiki, catching at ears as wildfire catches the boughs of trees, until the stories of Iakovos reached the port of Thessaloníki, whence they were seaborne and unstoppable.

In his palace at Blachernae, in the northeast of the City, the Emperor was hearing reports from the provinces. The news sickened him. He wandered to the window to see birds making their nests. Forever building and rebuilding: new life from the ruins of the old. 'And what of Thessalonica?' the Emperor asked. The reply was not a happy one.

'Oh but your Majesty,' said the counsellor, 'there is a story of an Athonite monk that might amuse you.'

So the Emperor learned of Iakovos who shone with divine

light, who flew to the mountaintop to speak with the Virgin and knew of things past, present and to come. The idea entered the Emperor's head to go on a pilgrimage to Athos. But his contracting empire was under assault from within and without. He could not leave his palace. He sent a priest with soldiers to bring the hermit to him.

Iakovos was at the monastery, receiving Holy Communion, when the delegation arrived. The hermit recognised the imperial ensign. He sat on the ground. The delegation had to carry him, unhindered but without help, the many miles to the port of Daphne.

What passed through the hermit's mind as the ramparts of the peninsula receded? Perhaps, as its monasteries dissolved in the sea haze, he prayed for the Intercession of the Virgin: 'Grant me, O Mother of God, a safe return to your mountain, that I may sing your glory there until the end of my days.' To the soldiers who had carried him, Iakovos seemed a nothing: a halfwit in the hold, munching his gums.

It was an anxious journey through the Dardanelles, with the captain at the prow, warily assessing each approaching sail. Iakovos, as he prayed below deck, did not see the conquered shores of Gallipolis, or the minarets rising on the coast of Ilium. He did not see, as for the hundredth time that hour he intoned the Jesus Prayer, the imperial fleet in the Sea of Marmara huddling stern-to-bow, nor the ancient walls of the Queen of Cities when at last they reached her harbour.

The priest sent to escort Iakovos found him shivering in the bilge waters. Throughout the voyage, the hermit had been jealous of his stillness and silence; he broke them now to request a covered carriage for the last part of his journey. He meant, doubtless, to hide himself from the city, though it was sure to peep through the curtains in smells and strange voices, in languages he had never heard, and the music, sweet and sinful, of a cimbalom.

The hermit – though he could be called that no longer

– was given furnished lodgings in the palace at Blachernae. In the morning when they summoned him, the ministers found his carpets, folding stool, his writing table and bed pushed to a far wall. Iakovos was reciting the third prayer of St Macarius the Great. He regarded the ministers as if they were moths or sparrows: a chance, windblown apparition.

The Emperor stood, respectful of holiness, when the old man entered the throne room. The Fool of God's wits were good enough for him to bow. He accepted a seat but refused any food. 'Your fame precedes you,' said the Emperor. 'I have heard wonderful tales of the Spirit working through you.'

Iakovos smiled benignly.

'You are said to shine with divine light,' said the Emperor, 'like Our Lord on Mount Tabor. Is this true? Tell me, Father, does it burn without or within? Can you feel the breath of the Holy Spirit? Are you afraid, or does it delight you?'

Iakovos was still, a pillar of flesh.

'I ask you to break your silence. My duties are all temporal: I can only approach the divine through holy men.'

Iakovos did not stir.

'Come!' said the Emperor and his jowls trembled. 'This folly is a mask behind which you shelter. I command you to speak.'

Iakovos sighed. His grey eyes met the black eyes of the Emperor. 'Is it spiritual instruction that His Majesty seeks? If so, the Patriarch of the City would serve his purpose. I am but a ragged old man, unfit even for monastic life, pining for the desert.'

'Speak to me,' said the Emperor, 'of what is past, present, and to come.'

Iakovos stared with the effrontery of old age. A gust of laughter left him. He began to sing the *Polyelaion*, smiling at the rafters where a trapped sparrow fluttered.

'Do not try to hide from me, Father. I must know what the future holds, that I may govern wisely.'

A change came over Iakovos. Every muscle in his old body

tautened. His eyes stared wide at a spot above the Emperor's head, his withered arms extended. 'You will die,' he said in a ghostly voice.

Ministers at the back of the room shuddered but the Emperor was not impressed. 'All men die. I do not need a holy man to tell me that. Specifics, come.'

Iakovos let his arms drop to his sides. 'How can I please your Imperial Majesty? Since the visions you claim I have are of the future, the future you claim I perceive can in no way be altered. Otherwise I would prophesy those changes.'

The Emperor grew angry at these evasions. The old man might belong to God but he was also a subject of the Empire.

'You would do no good with your foreknowledge,' said Iakovos. 'You would use it to shore up your strength, instead of saving your people. I refer, of course, to their immortal souls.'

Cursed for his manners, the old man was dismissed and returned to his lodgings. The Emperor ordered – against all decorum – that Iakovos be confined under lock and key, until he saw fit to discharge his duty.

A week passed before the second summons. The ministers found the old man kneeling in the stone centre of his cell, reciting a prayer of thanks for the noon meal. When he had finished praying, he followed them in silence.

One of the ministers, a man of little faith, whispered to another, 'If it is feigned, the Emperor will punish him by keeping him here, in the world that he loathes.'

'If it is *not* feigned,' said his colleague, 'His Highness will not wish to part with such an asset.'

With cold eyes, they watched the shambling hermit and contemplated laying a wager on the outcome.

Again, the Emperor stood to greet his guest; again, Iakovos bowed. 'I have waited seven days,' said the Emperor. 'Recognise my forbearance. You have only the burden of prayer. I have a thousand years on my back.'

'Would knowing the next thousand reduce the weight?'

The Emperor smiled with sour triumph. 'So you *can* speak when unbidden.'

'My lord, I beg leave to return to my desert.'

'Then prophesy,' said the Emperor.

Iakovos looked unhappily at the rafters. 'I have never claimed to have the gift.'

'The claim has been made for you.'

'And if it were true, your Greatness, you would not heed those things that do not suit your present purpose.'

'You are a charlatan!' The Emperor lifted himself, trembling, on the arms of his throne. 'You have no gift of foresight and dissemble the lack in pieties. Take him away, lest I damn myself by striking a man of God!'

So Iakovos was dismissed a second time. Back in his cell, those thick walls that kept out the summer heat kept out also the noise of the city.

Frustrated as he was, the Emperor did not despair of his prophet. The minister of little faith was summoned to his chambers.

'You will not prevail,' the minister said, 'by immuring him in the palace. Privation may loosen lay tongues but it is manna to the godly. Iakovos longs only for the desert. He would not withstand its opposite.'

Duly advised, the Emperor changed tactic. He ordered Iakovos to attend imperial ceremonies: those elaborate and sclerotic rites of half-forgotten meaning. He gave him, as befitted the old man's honour, a new suite filled with cushions and sweetmeats. He instructed a guide to lead Iakovos on tours of the City, and an armed guard was laid on to ensure his progress.

The strategy worked. Spies reported on the distress of the hermit as variety and disorder pressed in on him, stimulating his imagination and robbing him of the emptiness that is the laying aside of thoughts.

Somehow, one evening as the heat began to abate, the old man gave his escort the slip. Nobody dared inform the

Emperor. Search parties were sent out and sentries at every gate instructed to look for him. Darkness fell and a soldier stumbled on the steps of the church of the Theotokos. '*You*,' said the soldier as the obstacle groaned. Reciting the Prayer of Intercession to the Most Holy Mother of God, Iakovos was lifted from his chosen dwelling and escorted back to the palace.

The Emperor was restless in his bed, sleep and prayer elusive. He heard a troop of guards in the courtyard and went to look from his window. Moments later, he was robed and enthroned, waiting to hear from the prophet.

Iakovos was sweating, though it was cool in the marble throne room. Lank white hair plastered his forehead; his left hand distractedly trembled. 'Will it please your Majesty to restore an old man to his hermitage and the death that awaits him?'

'Tell me what you see, Father.'

'I see,' said Iakovos, 'the evaporation of your territories, as frost melts under the hot breath of the Sultan.'

The Emperor absorbed this and nodded. He became aware of prying eyes and ordered his ministers and servants to depart. When the door had closed on the last indignant lord, the Emperor beckoned the old man closer. 'When I seized back my throne from its usurper,' he said, 'I dreamed of becoming a second Justinian. Surely, what once was could become again? Yet under my rule we have lost Adrianople and Philoppolis, we have surrendered Serbia and been ousted from Gallipolis. And now I see that my dream was as the ant's dream of conquering the forest.'

At this confession the Emperor saw – or believed he saw – a strange glow in the old man's face.

'Your own fate,' said Iakovos.

'Tell me.'

'I see humiliation in a city of bridges. I see a lion beneath the paw of its cub…'

'What must I do?'

But Iakovos had passed into ecstasy. He no longer prayed but was carried by prayer as a raft is pulled by the current. His face shone like vellum held up to the sun, and from his carious mouth the Emperor heard what he already knew. 'The City will fall.'

'When?'

'I see barrels of iron spouting fire. I see ships travelling on land across the broken back of a forest. I see the breaking of icons, and minarets about the dome of Hagia Sophia.'

'Will this happen in my reign?'

But the prophet was not master of his visions. On they took him, across centuries: past flying ships and killing clouds to a world of drought and floods. Iakovos himself began to tremble at a vision of the Holy Mountain in flames. Its chestnut forests and hazel groves burned, great waves of fire engulfed Chilandari monastery and Grigoriou, Panteleimon and Great Lavra itself. Iakovos cried for release. The Emperor caught him as he fell.

The vision failed.

The light was extinguished.

For several minutes an onlooker, had there been one, would have seen majesty on its knees and an old man wiping the sweat from his brow as he muttered, 'Lord Jesus Christ, Son of God, have mercy upon me, a sinner.'

At last the Emperor spoke. 'Your prophecy leaves me quite without hope.'

'Hope, my lord? There is always a place for hope.'

'It would sap my people of resistance to know these things.'

Iakovos raised himself to his knees. 'Whether the End comes today or centuries hence,' he said, 'it is as a blink in the eye of God. I shall endeavour to believe that your concern is for the well-being of your subjects. Mine is only prayer and the readying of my soul for its final journey.'

Now Iakovos, hermit of the burning hut, requested his release. But the Emperor gave a cruel smile. 'Since you have the gift of prophesy,' he said, 'you know already what my answer must be. You carry in your head the destruction of the Empire. So you and your head shall remain in the City, until the vision is extinguished.'

Iakovos replied. 'It is a shadow you stamp on, great lord. That which casts the shadow is beyond your power.'

But already the Emperor was leaving, and guards with heavy tread were entering the throne-room with a duty to perform.

The Time Traveller's Breakdown

IT WAS SUPPOSED TO be a quick trip back to a familiar place: a preliminary jaunt, as if ninety years was no great distance, a hop down the road to the next town perhaps, where by dint of proximity to your starting place the dangers of getting marooned, lost without hope of recovery, were remote to non-existent. In hindsight – and there would be plenty of time for it, to the very edge of your own conception – it had been unwise to depart like this, experimentally, without putting in place contingency plans in case of malfunction or misadventure. As a boy, in a world you may live to see again, you had been warned, whenever you felt the lure of the heath, the call of the pinewoods, not to leave the house without informing others, your parents or neighbours, of the route that you intended taking, of the hour when you anticipated your return. Getting lost then had been a fearful prospect. Perhaps too you had longed for it, for the romance of blending into the land, of sinking or appearing to sink under the tides of bracken, the brittle tangles of ling. Once, aged ten, you had (and will again: there is the madness of it) concealed yourself for an afternoon in a sandy trench, with a covering of furze above you, the green exterior, the dead and tawny centre, thinking it a perfect hideaway, a refuge never to be discovered by your parents or other emissaries from the hateful world of adults. You had imagined yourself a thirsty stowaway on the sweltering ship of the hill, sitting out the summer, turning feral. You had imagined people calling your name, their voices muted by the bank that concealed you. You would not have responded to their cries: you would have stayed lost.

As later, decades beforehand, you surveyed that hiding place and knew you were lost beyond hope of recovery: the first and perhaps the only man to realise a fantastic dream. It had done you no good. Your machine was dead, a clutter of parts ninety years shy of the necessary replacements, pushed into a ditch beneath the poisoned shelter of a rhododendron. Before you realised where you were (if *where* can be another word for a predicament), you ran across the hills scouting out your discovery. For all had changed, or had not yet changed. The shape of the land was as you remembered, yet the serried ranks of Scots pine were missing, the hills were tousled with heather and birch, with here and there the scorched evidence of fires, the blackened soil sprouting, like green crystals in a Petri dish, the ancestors of remembered gorse. Stranger still was the absence of the motorway: in its place the old supposed wastes, the white pastures of unimproved grass, and low cottages such as Hardy might have known, with at their gates a surly, sun-browned people destined to vanish with their manners.

These people you avoided: the dangers of interference, that timeworn conceit of a thousand stories, seemed real enough now that you had accomplished the impossible. Besides, they would only have thought you mad and summoned a bobby from central casting to take you away in his buxom, antique car.

For hours, on that solitary day of your delight, you wandered where in the future housing estates would sprawl, the shopping malls with their dead meadows of parked cars, the fast-food outlets, the service stations, the lay-bys and garden centres, the generic motels and garages, the neon hangar of the out-of-town multiplex. It seemed to you that you visited the world in its innocence. There were still commoners gathering furze on the heath and putting their cattle out to graze. In the quiet, without the sounds of aircraft or road traffic on its endless loop, you could hear birds that would vanish with the century: a yellowhammer on a telegraph post, wood larks and nightjars, the crazed rattle of a Dartford warbler. Decriers of progress had a point: you had always known it.

You would come to regret the comforts of nostalgia. To go back is to invite utter desolation.

That first night, and then with deepening apprehension, what had seemed glorious to you became a torment. You were home, yet farther from home than it is possible to be. Unwilling to abandon hope, you kicked about the area, spending your diligently curated money in grocers and alehouses, racking your brains for a solution. The strangeness of your predicament gave you migraines – terrible, nauseating bouts that sent you reeling to the darkness of your vessel, where sleep would cram you into its mouth only to spit you out, when the pain subsided, into the monstrous paradox of your situation.

Perhaps the journey had done you neural damage; perhaps you were insane, for who understands the medical consequences of such travel, let alone the psychic jarring of going against nature? For a period you drifted on the floods of a fever. Inchoate dreams of heat and sand, the maculate shade of dry leaves above you, gave way as the fever abated to willed dreams of the life you had lost. Lucidly you took yourself from room to room in your apartment, in your workshop, taking in the play of light on the walls, the scuffs in the carpet and the stains above the hob, scrutinising all that was negligible, as if doing so might transport you home – to the world with you in it.

The delirium ceased. You stood empty-headed, parched and soiled on the borders of despair; yet you did not enter. You lived, you still lived, you could not stay, not here, waiting years for the familiar landmarks to appear: the roads, the houses, the looming struts and spires of the telecoms tower. Even as you suffered, enough curiosity survived in you to notice that it was this absence, the empty sky where the colossus used to stand training its red eye at the night, that distressed you more than anything, though you had feared the tower as a boy and hated it as a teenager, that inhuman sentinel watching for the missiles that would mean the end of everything. Now that the tower, and the dread that it embodied, were gone, or not yet come, you grieved at the thought that, if you survived, you would not see it restored to its place above the common until you were on your last legs.

You took leave of the heath – stumbling one hot day down a dusty track to the gates of a country house sheltered by trees: shaggy elms and pines and stately cedars. You knew the place; or rather, you did not know it for certain until, by following the iron fence, you found the smallholding, the diminutive nursery from which a copper beech would emerge to shade your childhood reading; and there, the chickens that would give your parents the only good soil on the housing estate, the very spot where the family home would stand.

There was nothing else for your pilgrimage. Only one building which you looked for, your jaw clenched so tightly that the pain when you released it in the evening would make you howl. You found the old barn. Not so old, though abandoned already. Entered like a disciple his prophet's tomb. Searched out the corner where as a boy you would sit and watch the drifting motes, the sun's latticework on the rafters. Wanting that familiar wall behind you, inhaling that familiar air. With your eyes shut, with the murmur of bees outside, it was possible for a delirious instant to make that homeward journey, as though you had only to dream to find yourself back again, to that place in the future. It was bitter to open your eyes on a present not yet peopled with those you loved. Behind you, no girlfriend's name was etched into the brick.

Vagrancy was your only option. For fear of warping history, you fled the places where people lived, reducing to a minimum your interactions, making the open road your home. To preserve your funds, which had to last, you skulked along hedgerows, slept under bridges, took shelter from the rain in the ruins of upland farms. Mercifully you had not left behind loved ones to mourn your disappearance. The thought occurred to you that you had family living, though it would not know you. To go there: to be near flesh and blood, offering yourself as a gardener to your great-grandparents, or simply falling into step behind a maid and her perambulator in the park. But it could not be. You must not tamper – though even breathing, in a place where nature had not sent you, risked a chain reaction. Unless, that is, your blunder into the past had already occurred when you were born – would always occur, and your later self had already existed, would *always* exist, in the place before you came to it. Shipwrecked on the shores of your prehistory, you wrestled with the dangers; and perhaps because survival hinged upon the conclusions, you determined that you had always been here, that it would be safe to mingle, albeit unobtrusively, with the world.

Even so, the consolations of love had to be rejected. Not that many women would have looked at you. A drifter, inattentive of your looks and stubbled with anonymity, you laboured in a vineyard in Languedoc, you farmed sheep on the Cumbrian fells. A sour and taciturn creature, mystic to some and madman to others, you never stayed long in one place. A nomad, some said. A tramp, said others, who detected in ways they could not have spoken the unfitting odour of one of nature's outcasts.

Survivors of disaster imagine their existence to be posthumous, but you were premature, an untimely ghost. At times you flirted with temptation: to place that seemingly reckless bet on a sure-fire derby winner, to seek out the indigent artist offering his paintings in exchange for supper. A less scrupulous man might have exploited his advantages, but not you; you admired yourself for it, the satisfaction of your moral grandeur weakened only by the lack of another to appreciate it – unless you counted God, in whom your hopes

have always been slender. To be watched, to know that you are
watched, even loved, you spoke to yourself: you were your
surest friend. With strangers you spoke of yourself in the third
person, while they listened, or pretended to listen, their eyes
sidling across your shoulder. People learned to shun you in the
queue for work, in the bathhouse, in the shuffling line of
paupers waiting for soup and bread.

Several times, impelled by loneliness, you wandered back
to the heath. You inspected a young forest of regimented pines;
you watched as the army commandeered the common,
chasing the last furze-cutters from its tank-scoured slopes. You
recognised with grim satisfaction the concrete bunkers
erected, as you knew they would be, for the training of soldiers.
And you saw it all: the millions burning and yet to burn, the
subjugation of nations, fifty years of darkness descending and
you powerless to stop any of it.

There is little left to recount. One day it dawned on you
that your father had come into the world. In another year your
mother followed. Those whom you had buried breathed the
sweet air. This brought you comfort as you wore out the last
of your strength building cheerless homes unfit for heroes.

Vagrancy and official inexistence left you no pension. With
only a few savings, you returned to the place where you began;
you came back to the pines and heather, finding all closer to
what you remembered: the roads built, the new and vaunted
motorway bringing noise and litter and fanning flames from
discarded cigarettes across the common. You knew that these
things were in the past: they were long gone, no more than
pictures in a book. There was no sense in regretting them.

You took a room in a crumbling pub on the main road
through the village. Somewhere in the hills the remains of
your craft lay, though you had forgotten the precise location.

Why did you stay? What were you waiting for? You had no
hobbies, no interests. You could summon no energy to watch
history in the form of current affairs. All that remained was an

occasional stroll, slow and hacking of breath, up to the derelict country house.

Watching from a bench across the lane the churning up of the soil, the vacancy of the cottage garden and the felling of inconvenient trees, you felt the stirrings of a last obsession. All summer and autumn you watched as the houses went up. You saw, trembling with absurd hope of, what − rescue? salvation? − your own home, your childhood home, go up for sale and receive its visitors. And soon, quite soon, before the developers had finished their meagre plantings, you came in rain and sorrow to your tramp's throne on the rotting bench and saw that the 'For Sale' notice had been taken down and the place had been sold and a familiar Citroen sat gaping on the driveway while its owners carried in their few possessions.

What happens now? Will you cease at the instant of your conception, swallowed up by paradox? Or might you, like St Simeon, hold an infant in your arms and pray for your dismissal? Will your parents let you hold yourself and solder the loop of an eternal recommencement? For that child in turn will watch itself, when it has repeated your mistake, your remarkable disaster.

Go then. Go. You know, from your earliest clambering days, the perfect spot from which to spy on them. Beneath the dry ribs of that already ancient laurel. You can crouch there. You will crouch, staring through leaves like a famished animal. She will be in the garden, putting out the washing (you know this already: you have heard the story). You will watch her putting out their clothes to dry. And perhaps she will hear something, or an undreamt of sense will kindle in her unworked womb, for she will make you out in your hiding-place. Surprised, unnerved, she will venture as calmly as surface can seem into the house; where she will summon her husband, telling him what she has seen, and he will decide, after some hesitation but wanting to be manly, to confront you in the bushes.

'Hallo there. Hallo.'

You will crawl out at the summons. Your throat will be parched, as though the walls of it are fastened with needles. You will watch this boy, barely old enough to be married, who addresses you.

'Can I help you?'

Upon meeting his eyes you will lower your own. The dry parchment of your hand will tremble against your brow. Your father, whom last you saw in a broken body, regarding you with caution, an attempt perhaps at pity.

'Are you from the old house?'

'No.'

'We've just moved in.'

'I have waited.'

Your mother, reassured somewhat and wanting to rescue her husband, will join you on the gravel path. You will begin to shake, palsied with grief. This is too much: you will mutter like a drunk, will stink like one too.

'We understand,' the man will say, 'that this used to be a country estate. You must have seen some changes.'

You will turn your back. You will turn your back on them and look across your shoulder once. And they will stare at you, their impossible son, as you shuffle off to death and the birth that awaits you.

The Halt

FFAAHH! I'M STILL TOP dog, don't forget. There's the whole pile of them, a tawdry bleeding mess I tell you, under my club. I can feel them straining. Well it can't be comfortable, what with the dark and the cramped conditions. First there's the crush, and the stink. Then the humiliation.

I hope they're in agony.

As for me, there's one comfort in this shit hole. By comfort I don't mean a cushion for me noggin and cotton wool up me bum. I'm talking Philosophy. I'm talking Theology. Because there's an order to things, a proper ordering. It's why I'm top of the roost and they're at the bottom eating sawdust. No, you won't see me down there with the copper, with the hangman. From the summit you can think for miles. It's what I do, I don't rush. I remember everything as it was, in the beginning. Out in the light. The Hand that moves, the Swazzle that speaks. And me with my club, sermonising. Listen. There was waiting and sleeping and hanging around. It wasn't all nag and bludgeon. But at least you knew what was coming, there were things to look forward to. The very worst that happened was only a halt, which meant more of the same to come.

First sounds were the crowd and the breathing sea. Then in the darkness it would tickle and tingle, I could feel it, the Hand. And suddenly – ffffaaahh! Twitching into action, with the Swazzle speaking through me, with the Eyes and Light on me! Oh the battering! The nagging and the beating! Going at the baby with my club, yes, pinning the nipper to the ledge

177

and pulping him *bam-bam-bam* till he's dead. What larks! And still bashing when he's limp. Smack his curly bonce! Cream his gaping cakehole! Now the wife comes in, screaming blue murder. (The fuss she made about the nipper! It was a right bastard, her rolling-pin, and she wasn't shy using it.) Before I can shut her trap the copper appears. Ullo ullo he says and up flicks a truncheon. Well I'm having none of it, I smash his purple rotten face. Next up's the hangman. I don't just beat him, not always. Sometimes, when the Hand is most dancing in me, I stuff his neck in the noose and let him dangle. Then, when the doctor runs in, I crush his poxy mush. Take that, sawbones! I tell you, I had the run of the place. Only the priest, I wasn't allowed to bash the priest. Not his pious stinking mug, not his pious stinking conk. I should have been free to smash his bonce but the Hand wouldn't have it. No, no, the priest was the last straw. If I went for him (and I always went for him) up would come the bleeding crocodile, licking his bleeding chops. And then, what larks! Mangled in his stinking teeth! I don't know what was going on between the priest and that crock, some kind of racket that's for sure. As for Beelzebub, I could have taken him on. That pitchfork for my club? There was no contest. And those puny wooden horns! I mean in a straight fight, paddle to paddle, what was he going to do, gore me? Listen, I'd have shoved those pointy pricks up his stinking arse given half the chance. But the chance was never given.

Now I don't ask for much, not any more. Just one more fight up the beastly Congo, with my disciples all around me. Wherever I fought they followed, even into the fiery furnace. What days! With the Hand working through me, with the Swazzle! Instructing the young in the ways of battery.

But all that's gone. We rot in the dark in this place. Lost, if not forgotten. It doesn't change my standing, mind. It doesn't mean I don't exist. How can I squash the others if I don't exist?

But I don't move, I can't move, not a fucking paddle!

Funny thing is, I still feel it sometimes. Like now, right now, the Hand in my head. In my right arm, the Little Finger.

In my left, where my club lives, the Thumb. And lastly (the Hand being fivefold), Middle and Ring, bowing. I know it's there, the Hand. I feel it, don't I? And if the Hand is there, so are the Eyes. My disciples on the strand, gawking and clapping. And the gleaming Teeth, that are legion.

All I ask is a twitch. A shiver. Some sign that I'm not forsaken.

But there it is, you make do. You have to. I've got my routine. Count the pile beneath me. Bottom up, top down, whichever way you look at it, I'm still the boss. Then I make anagrams of my name, of their names. Say them back to front, mix them up, put them back together again — what do you get? Me coming out tops, not changed one jot since my old triumphs. When I left a trail of death. Corpses on hooks, with their bonces hanging. Laughter roaring like blood in my head. It was my day, even the dog knew it, with his tail wagging and the cap between his jaws. Listen. I'll tell you. The day is coming, I can feel it. The day is coming when the Hand will rise again. There will be a Lifting of the Darkness and Light shall have dominion. Then the Hand and the Swazzle shall take possession of my body. And the Reign of my Club will last a thousand years.

★

With only words to work on I haven't a hope. It's there, polished and solid, the means of my death. In my head. Oh but it is ingenious, my machine, in its ideal booth. Activated by my feet, which now stare white and dumbly at the rest of me. Incidentally my feet do a little turn, not a geometrical turn, every so often, when they think I'm not looking. Offering, in the sheets, a spasmodic gesture. Because I may seem a little distant, it's true, a trifle out-of-sorts, but I am still all there. I'm not all *here* of course, not by any stretch of the imagination. I'm here and there, roundabout. Scattered. I wonder, by the way, is there a special cemetery for the purpose, or several, divided along anatomical lines, with box hedges, or yew, and maybe privet for cocks and balls? Did they hold a service, I wonder? Were there asphodels and lilies? So many questions I would ask, of my draughtsman for instance. How could they refuse me a draughtsman, in my condition? I call him Tom, a fine fellow, you couldn't think of a finer. He comes when I summon him, to lend a hand, both hands to be honest, to sketch and design the means of my death. Let me show you the booth. Not the old one, which I carried on my back on the shingle, with its blue and red-striped canvas and the stays for my, for me to rest on during the performance. No, I'm referring to the booth for my machine, the black booth where I shall die, all being well, strapped to my contraption. It is hooded, though not to keep the rain out, and sealed once I'm inside, with my puppets. I sit on a stool with their ashes on my lap. My intact and self-satisfied feet are fastened to the pedals. The pedals drive the pump which is attached to the booth, with vents coming in. With regards to the booth, I would draw your attention to ventilation. It must be airtight, that not a puff of gas go wasting, for economy's sake. What happens afterwards, either to myself or the booth, or to what remains of my puppets, is not my concern. Yet I must say, if I am honest, that I regret the limitations of my system, for it is not perfect, oh no, not by any stretch of the imagination. I am referring, naturally, to the problem of restricted view, from an audience perspective. Children, the little shriekers, who are welcome by the way to attend if it pleases them, complained often enough, in the old days, of the old booth. Sometimes they sat too low, sometimes too far away. Even Toby was prone to making mistakes, I mean blocking the sightlines, with his doggy antics. On one occasion I remember a little boy pulled him from the stage. He was within easy reach, the vermin, I took great pleasure collecting that ginger clump of hair. Young Toby is dead now, long dead, his little bag and growl are buried, we shall not look on his ruff again. But of the booth, where was I, the booth, it is black, did I mention? Yes, entirely black, it does put one in mind of a confessional. A fairground confessional, perhaps, with a priest who says prayers for thruppence and absolves you from his coin-slot maw. Now there's an idea you could patent and sell to Rome! Automata fathers, confessing the world two up from Punch and Judy. For it doesn't take, I can tell you, live preachers to stir young souls when all the world has lost its head. We bought it, didn't we, the whole damn shooting match! We lined up and pretended we were men, with all that implies, of Freedom and Will. But we died as boys. We twitched in their hands, every man Jack, in their white-gloved hands that drew arrows in pencil on maps, hands that pointed from posters that I pasted onto my booth, the old booth that is, with its red and blue-striped canvas. But of the performance, the performance pending I mean, for let us be practical. We have the booth, that much is settled, and the pump and the stool. As for gas, I've settled on carbon monoxide. It's an excellent choice, believe me. You can't see it yet it's there, in any exhaust you care to mention, going unnoticed and too often to waste. Let me tell you about going unnoticed. It was always my forte, being incognito I mean. Now the booth, on the shingle, people tended to notice the booth. And the puppets, going about their jolly slaughter. But the Professor inside? Im-poss-ib-le to see. Now, here, in this bed, in this ward, in this bed, I am once more im-poss-ib-le to see. The nurses work around me and despite me. Others in the ward can still groan a little. Those without feet can take a pinch of rump. As for me, I can scowl I suppose, if this is still a scowl. But frankly, short of kicking a nurse up the crotch, which would require some planning on account of the sheets, what can I do except breathe with intent? But of the booth. But of the booth and the acquiring of materials, I mean once the draughtsman has finished, according to my specifications, the blueprint for the booth and the pump and the pedals. You may be wondering how I propose to get into it, ingress being precluded by the absence, for the gas, of any means of egress.

In the old booth I simply entered from below, shrugging it on like a shirt. But that assumed arms, to do the lifting, as indeed everything assumes arms, for most activities, and if you have a face and shoulders and both eyes to boot, so much the better. But of the booth, that's the black one, I propose to hire a man for the purpose. A bottler, if you like, for lifting the booth, to assist my entry, and a second man, or maybe a woman, don't think of that, to help me find the stool or the stool find me. Then when I am installed in my contraption the man, the booth-lifter that is, will lower the booth over me, taking care to seal it to the floor with pitch, or if not with pitch, for the sake of the hospital carpet, sealing-wax. I will have my puppets with me, which I will have had burned, a feeble heap of cinders in my lap. Because the gas cannot do for them what it does for me. All I will need for the burning is a crowbar, with human operator, to prize the box open. Then some paraffin. Matches, not too many, and a match-striker, naturally, to get the flame going. I remember the order I packed them in, my puppets, folded like pajamas one on top of another. On the left side of the box, because on the right are the scrolls, of various backdrops, unfurlable scenes depicting an African swamp, the ninth circle of Hell, Sweeney Todd's barbershop and a haunted castle. But of the puppets, in what order are they packed? The doctor, the policeman, the crocodile, the hangman, the devil, no, the baby. The baby then the hangman then the devil. The devil, the policeman, the crocodile, the priest or is it Judy? No, the priest, then Judy then Toby, not Toby, then the baby. Who've I missed? They're all there, anyway, in the box beneath my bed. They showed it to me some weeks ago, my box, thinking to be kind. At the time the infection screen was up, hiding my losses. Like a tent it was, all poles and canvas. White, off-white. A little white booth, the second of three. And my arms were somewhere inside, I could feel them. I can still feel them, what do surgeons know? They're not up to much, mind you, awful bloody fists. I ask them kindly, could they unclench please, please could they

unclench, please? In the first days, under my tent, I would
have sent them in quest of absent parts. But I couldn't get a
message down the line. God oh God!

As we were, concerning the puppets. I used to drop them,
Punch's victims, out of the booth. Sometimes they flopped and
sometimes I flung them with great violence. The puppets were
dead, you see, and something in their trajectory shocked my
audience. They didn't hoot at play going awry. The lifeless
effigies fell into their world. Out of the fabulous. And silenced
them all. But, you want to know about the contraption. How
to build it, the whole machine that is. How to kill a man who
is, by most of the usual standards, pretty much dead already.
Certainly it's a fair question, leaving aside the ethics of the
matter, for I do need assistance. My purpose, in making the
booth, is you understand to make entirely sure of a successful
end. I mean an end to immobility and an end to invisibility. I
don't pretend there are not mighty obstacles to surmount, men
in conditions like mine are hard to destroy. Ask any soldier, the
healthy ones you can snap like a twig. It's no momentous
matter. Mostly, if you kill anyone, you fire at a puff of smoke,
a jerking figure in the distance. One second twitching in the
parabola of the sight. Then not. And that's how men die in
battle. No balletic grace, no aesthetic gesture. A hand
withdrawn from a glove. But of the booth, but of the booth, I
am so easily distracted, my words wander. We were in a
foxhole, stupid bloody name for it, Jimmy and me. Jimmy had
a hole where his jaw used to be. I could hear him breathing, it
was a gargle, like a man rinsing his mouth after supper. It was
dark, I put my finger in and felt a top row of teeth. The tongue
stub twitched. I didn't want to see his eyes, they were rolling,
I didn't want to see them. But of the booth. But of the booth,
the black one, you're growing impatient. I couldn't take it, I
scrabbled away from him. Even with my hands on my ears I
could hear him. With my fingers in my ears, podged into the

vents, I could still hear Jimmy gasping. His hands trembling like a loom. I should have shot him. All night he stroked the slope with his heels, until morning curled him up and he stopped. Little Jimmy with his sweetheart in his pocket. Quite chapfallen. I was lucky, in comparison, having none alive to mourn me, for what's the use of a darling's tears when you're dead and disassembled? As I was, two days later, disassembled. We'd taken an enemy trench. In the midst of triumph, disaster! An ingenious contraption it was, I could learn much from its maker. In fact, when it comes to the technology of the booth, I mean to applying it in practice, he might be the very man for the job. You should have seen his handiwork. So should I! Hair-thread trigger attached to the lid. A good bottle of brandy going to waste. The medics reached me quickly. They did too good a job of keeping me alive. Who now cannot see me. But I don't blame them, really I don't. If I could speak I would tell them so. For there is no contraption. There is no pump. There are no pedals. There is no Tom, no angel of mercy. There is only this bed, this hospital bed, and this head. A head that troubles no one but me. For inanimate things cannot suffer, it stands to reason. Only now there are holes in my head through which the wind blows, making a sound. I cannot hear it but it's there. Like my hands. In spite of physical evidence. The sound of the wind all the same.

About the Author

Gregory Norminton's novels include *The Ship of Fools* (2002), *Arts and Wonders* (2004), *Ghost Portrait* (2005) and *Serious Things* (2008), all published by Sceptre. Other books include *The Lost Art of Losing* (2012), *Thumbnails* (2013) and *Beacons: Stories for Our Not So Distant Future* (editor, 2013). His stories have appeared on BBC Radio 4, and in *Prospect, Resurgence, London Magazine* and *The Lonely Crowd*. He teaches Creative Writing and English at Manchester Metropolitan University.

www.gregorynorminton.co.uk